'No?' She lau
'Come on, Ada
guts to tell me
know that you didn
along on this trip and we both
know why, too.'

'And that has nothing to do with my decision. I'm in charge of this team and it's up to me what happens.'

'Then why won't you leave me in charge of this patient?'

'Because it's too dangerous, that's why!'

He swung round and she took a step back when she saw the anger in his eyes.

Yet she knew on some inner level that it wasn't directed at her but at himself.

'I am simply not prepared to put your life at risk, Kasey. And if you don't like it then there isn't much I can do, because nothing you say or do will make me change my mind.'

'I didn't realise…'

It seemed too incredible to believe after what had gone on between them, yet there wasn't a doubt in her mind that he was telling her the truth.

Dear Reader

I have always been fascinated by the work that is carried out by overseas aid agencies, and really admire the courage and dedication of the brave doctors and nurses who volunteer to help other people under the most arduous conditions. Setting up my own fictional medical aid agency is my tribute to them.

The people who work for Worlds Together do so for many different reasons, but mainly because they want to help save lives. In this book surgeon Adam Chandler intends to do all he can to help the people of Mwuranda. He has hand-picked his team of volunteers and is confident that everyone going on this mission is the cream of the crop. It comes as a shock when one of his anaesthetists drops out and he is forced to accept the services of Kasey Harris.

Kasey isn't sure why she volunteered to go to Mwuranda. She knows that Adam will give her a rough ride after she broke off their relationship, but she feels it's time that they let bygones be bygones. However, it soon becomes apparent that she will have her work cut out if she wants to end the hostilities between them. What she has never anticipated is that working with Adam will arouse feelings which she's tried to keep buried...

I really enjoyed helping Kasey and Adam work through their problems. However, no matter how difficult and dangerous their job is, it's nothing compared to finally facing their true feelings for one another.

Watch out for more books in my Worlds Together series in the coming months.

Best wishes

JENNIFER TAYLOR

THE FOREVER ASSIGNMENT

BY
JENNIFER TAYLOR

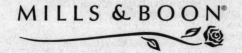

All the characters in this book have no existence outside the imagination of the author, and have no relation whatsoever to anyone bearing the same name or names. They are not even distantly inspired by any individual known or unknown to the author, and all the incidents are pure invention.

First published in Great Britain 2005
Harlequin Mills & Boon Limited,
Eton House, 18-24 Paradise Road, Richmond, Surrey TW9 1SR

© Jennifer Taylor 2005

ISBN 0 263 84329 7

Set in Times Roman 10½ on 11½ pt.
03-0905-55703

Printed and bound in Spain
by Litografia Rosés, S.A., Barcelona

CHAPTER ONE

'No!'

Adam Chandler slammed his hand down on the desk. It was rare that he ever lost his temper and he could see the surprise on people's faces as they turned to see what was happening.

The office was packed that day with members of his team and every single one of them had been hand-picked by him for their skills. Joan Simpson, for instance, was one of the world's leading authorities on dengue fever—a virulent tropical disease—while Gordon Thompson knew more about typhus than any person alive.

Adam's own speciality was reconstructive surgery and he knew without a shred of vanity that there were few people who could match him. This team was the cream of the crop and it had taken him months to put it together so it had been a huge blow when one of their anaesthetists had gone down with appendicitis the previous day. They were due to fly out to Mwuranda the following night and finding a replacement at such short notice had not been an easy task, so he'd been delighted when Shiloh Smith, the head of Worlds Together—the aid agency which was funding the trip—had phoned to tell him that he'd found the ideal candidate to go with them.

Adam had been on his way to Theatre at the time so he'd asked Shiloh to call at his office that afternoon and let him have the details then. There would be a lot of paperwork that would need to be completed before the newcomer could travel with them but he'd been confident he could get it done in time. Everything had been working out perfectly, in fact, until Shiloh had arrived and dropped his bombshell.

'There is no way that I'm taking Kasey Harris along on this trip.'

'That's what she said you'd say.' Shiloh laughed. 'OK, so what's the story? Do I take it that you two have a history?'

'Ask Kasey,' Adam replied shortly, standing up. He poured himself a cup of coffee, hoping Shiloh couldn't tell how rattled he was. He and Kasey most definitely had a history although it wasn't something he was prepared to discuss even with his oldest friend.

'I already did and she gave me the same answer as you just did.' Shiloh grinned. 'I'm starting to build up a picture here. Do I take it that you and the lovely Dr Harris were rather more than colleagues at one point?'

'You can take it any damn way you like,' Adam retorted, refusing to be drawn into talking about that episode in his life.

He picked up the cup and carried it back to his desk, thinking about what had happened five years ago. He had fallen head over heels in love with Kasey Harris, had honestly believed that she had been in love with him, too, but he'd been wrong. She had simply *used* his feelings as a way to pay him back for what she'd believed he'd done to her brother and it was hard to accept that he'd been so gullible. He'd never been someone who allowed his emotions to run away with him but, as he had discovered to his cost, love made fools of even the sanest people. The thought did little to soothe him and he glowered at the other man.

'My relationship with Kasey Harris isn't open for discussion. Understand?'

'OK. I get the message but it looks like we have a major problem on our hands, then.'

Shiloh sighed as he placed a sheet of paper on the desk. Adam tried not to look at it because he didn't want to see the photograph that was stapled to the top left-hand corner.

His eyes slid sideways before he could stop them and heat roared along his veins when he saw Kasey's face smiling up at him—that porcelain-fine skin, those deep blue eyes, that luscious mouth…

He dragged his gaze away and took a slug of coffee, relishing the way it scalded his tongue because it was easier to deal with physical pain than this mental torture. Shiloh was speaking again and he forced himself to concentrate on the most important issue which was finding another anaesthetist.

'So we're really stretched,' Shiloh concluded. 'As you know, we don't usually run two missions together but we had no choice in this instance. We'd just received permission for you to take your team into Mwuranda when there was all that flooding in Guatemala. Once the Guatemalan government declared it a national disaster, we immediately sent out a team.'

'I understand how difficult it is,' Adam assured him. 'But there must be someone else on your books.'

'I wish there was but we've lost several key people recently for one reason or another so we're having to recruit some new volunteers. Kasey's application only came in last month and I have to admit that I was impressed when I interviewed her. She's bright, personable and she knows her job, too. She's just the sort of person we need, in fact.'

'I'm not doubting her professional capabilities,' he ground out. 'I just don't want to have to work with her.'

'Then, as I said, we have a major problem. You need another anaesthetist to make this trip viable and there isn't anyone else available. It's your choice, Adam, but either you take her with you or you call off the trip.'

'Some choice,' Adam snorted because if he didn't take

the team to Mwuranda tomorrow as planned, there might not be another opportunity. There'd been civil unrest within the country for the past two years and there was no way of knowing how long the current ceasefire would last. He knew what a dire state the country was in because he'd witnessed it at first hand. The people there were desperately in need of medical aid—was he really prepared to stand aside and watch them suffer because he couldn't deal with what had happened in the past?

'It appears I don't have much option,' he said bitterly, glaring at the photograph. 'If it's a question of taking Kasey Harris along or not going, I'll just have to grin and bear it, won't I? But I want it put on record that I'm not happy about having her on my team.'

'My, my, but your enthusiasm is overwhelming, Adam. You could sweep a girl right off her feet with that attitude.'

His head reared up when he recognised the gently lilting voice. Just for a moment it felt as though the whole room was spinning out of focus before his eyes settled on the woman standing in front of his desk. She looked exactly like her photograph, he thought sickly—slim, elegant, her lustrous black hair curling around her face, her blue eyes gleaming with laughter. Or was it tears that made them shimmer that way?

Adam rose unsteadily to his feet, almost as shocked by that idea as he was to see her. Kasey had never cried. Not once. Not even when he'd told her what he'd thought of her. He hadn't held back, either, the words ripping out of him and into her, driven by pain and humiliation and sheer mind-numbing anguish. She had just stood there as the words rained down on her and smiled, and that had been his abiding memory all these years, the one that had caused him all those nightmares. Kasey Harris had smiled while she'd broken his heart.

*   *   *

Kasey held her smile but she knew how much it cost her even if Adam didn't. It had been a shock when Shiloh had told her who was leading this mission, so much so that she'd almost backed out. But then it had struck her that if she refused to go, Adam would have won.

She'd made enough changes to her life in the past five years because of him and it was time to stop. She had to draw a line under what had happened even if she still hadn't forgiven him for what he'd done to her brother. She doubted if Adam had forgiven her for what she'd done to *him* either, but that hadn't been the issue until she'd walked into his office and heard what he'd said. Maybe it was silly to have let the harsh words upset her, but they had.

'Come, come, Adam. It's not like you to be lost for words,' she taunted because she hated to admit that she was vulnerable in any way. She might regret why she'd had to do what she had but she didn't regret the outcome. Adam had deserved everything he'd got after the appalling way he'd treated Keiran!

'It isn't. Obviously, you've scored one up on me, Kasey. Satisfied?'

His sardonic tone mocked her and she felt the angry colour run up her cheeks. It took every scrap of control she possessed not to tell him to go to hell and march straight out of the room only she wouldn't give him the satisfaction of thinking he'd scared her off.

'It will do for a start,' she said sweetly. 'But I've never been one for resting on my laurels, as you know.'

His face darkened, the strong bones settling into such grim lines that a tremor ran through her. Adam had always been a force to be reckoned with and time had merely intensified that air of authority he possessed. He looked big and tough as he stood there glaring at her, his dark hair brushed smoothly back from his forehead, his green eyes piercing right to her very soul. He'd always been a handsome man and he still was, but there was no softness about him, no *give*, either in appearance or manner. He never compromised, never backed down, never showed any sign of weakness...apart from that night when she'd told him who she was.

The memory still had the power to disturb her so Kasey pushed it to the back of her mind as she turned to Shiloh. 'I thought it would save time if I brought my documents over here. Everything is sorted out now—visa, official notification from the Foreign Office to say that I'm a member of the Worlds Together team, vaccination certificates, etcetera.'

'Excellent!'

Shiloh smiled warmly at her, his welcoming attitude such a contrast to Adam's that she couldn't suppress the twinge of regret that speared through a corner of her heart. In other circumstances, she knew that she and Adam could have been friends but what had happened had ruled out that possibility. Just for a moment she found herself wondering if she had been mad to agree to spend the next month working with him. He would give her a rough ride, she wasn't in any doubt of that. So was it worth putting herself under that kind of pressure to prove a point? She opened her mouth to explain that she'd changed her mind only Adam chose that very moment to speak.

'I'm surprised you decided to join the agency. It doesn't strike me as your sort of thing at all, Kasey.'

'No?' Her delicate brows arched as she turned to him. 'Why not?'

'From what I remember, you always enjoyed the good things in life—dining out, exotic holidays, beautiful clothes.' His eyes skimmed over her, taking stock of the expensive black trouser suit she was wearing that day, and he laughed. 'I do hope you know what you're letting yourself in for.'

'You mean I won't be able to wear my Gucci loafers and Chanel suits while we're in Mwuranda?' She gasped in feigned horror. 'Heavens above! How will I cope?'

'Not very well with that attitude.' His smile disappeared in a trice. 'This isn't a game. There's been civil war in the country for the past two years and conditions there are about as bad as they can get. The people we will be treating have nothing left apart from their dignity and they certainly don't need you making jokes at their expense.'

'And you really think I need you to tell me that?' She took a step towards him, incensed by his patronising manner. 'I'm fully aware how bad the conditions are going to be, Adam. I've read the reports and I know what we'll be dealing with.'

'Do you really?' He laughed softly, scorn lacing his deep voice so that she winced inwardly. 'You may think you know what it's like to work in a country where the whole infrastructure has broken down but until you experience the reality for yourself, you can't possibly understand. It's going to be tough—really tough—and I'm not sure you're up to it.'

'Then we shall just have to wait and see who's right, won't we?' she said lightly. Maybe she didn't have any experience of working under such extreme conditions but she'd cope. She had to because the alternative to letting him think she was beaten wasn't an option. No matter how bad it was, she was going to complete this mission and show Adam *bloody* Chandler that he was wrong about her!

'I'm sure Kasey understands it won't be a picnic,' Shiloh said soothingly. 'Although, you're quite right to worry, Adam, because it's your job to ensure the safety and welfare of your team. However, let's not get side-tracked at the moment. I'm afraid we have another problem to sort out. Your flights are all arranged but there's been a bit of a hitch with the cargo.'

Kasey excused herself as the two men started to confer. She glanced around the room, wondering if she should introduce herself to the other members of the team. Shiloh had explained that they'd decided to hold a last-minute meeting to discuss any concerns the group might have and it might be an idea to let them know who she was. She made her way over to the corner where a group of women was standing and smiled at them.

'Hi! I'm Kasey Harris. I'm stepping in as a last-minute replacement for one of your anaesthetists.'

'Welcome aboard, Kasey.' One of the women immediately drew her into the group. 'I'm June Morris, one of the nurses. I keep saying I'm never going on another of these little jaunts but here I am again!'

Kasey laughed. 'You must enjoy it.'

'Enjoy being bitten by mozzies and sucked dry by leeches?' June rolled her eyes. 'Only a masochist would enjoy what we do, eh, girls?'

The other women laughed as Kasey grinned at them. 'OK, so why do you do it? Is it the excitement of working in a new place, or the buzz of being able to make a difference to people's lives?'

'Probably a mixture of both,' one of the women replied. She held out her hand. 'I'm Katie Dexter, by the way, another of June's little flock.'

'Nice to meet you.' Kasey shook hands. 'So that's two nurses so far. How many more of you are there?'

'Just Lorraine and Mary.' June explained, introducing the other two women. 'We could have done with a couple more, to be honest, but Adam has been very choosy. He only wanted people with experience of working in the field along on this trip.'

Kasey grimaced. 'Mmm, so I gathered.'

'He didn't seem too happy about you coming along,' Katie put in hesitantly, and June laughed.

'That's an understatement if ever I heard one! I never thought I'd see the day when Adam Chandler lost his cool. He's the proverbial ice-man but he hit the roof when Shiloh told him you were going to be on the team. Do I sense a juicy story?'

'Not really.' Kasey shrugged, trying to make light of what had gone on because she'd never told anyone what had happened between her and Adam. It wasn't that she was ashamed of what she'd done but she wasn't exactly proud of it either.

She sighed because it had all seemed so simple in the beginning, too. Her sole aim had been to show Adam that he couldn't go around playing god with people's lives the way he'd done with her brother. She'd decided to teach him a lesson he wouldn't forget. She'd known about Adam's reputation for being aloof, of course. Several of her friends had worked with him and they'd told her that he never mixed socially with his staff, but she hadn't let that deter her. Someone had needed to show him how it felt to have your whole life torn apart. So she'd got herself a job at the hospital where he'd worked with the express intention of trying to foster a relationship between them and, in the event, it had been surprisingly easy to do.

Kasey shivered. Even now she could recall the shock of their first meeting, still remember the way her skin had tingled when he'd shaken her hand and how her body had responded to the gravelly sound of his voice. That Adam had been equally affected hadn't been in any doubt, and it had scared her because it had been the last thing she'd expected, yet there had been no way that she could have backed out at that point. So she'd gone ahead with her plan—accepted his invitation to dinner the following night—even though she'd had qualms about what she'd been doing.

She'd been right to have doubts, too, she thought wryly, because it had soon become apparent that the situation was getting out of hand. Within the space of a few weeks, she realised that their feelings for one another were far deeper than she'd expected them to be and decided to call a halt. After all, she'd achieved her objective, so there was no reason to carry on, yet telling Adam the truth that night had been the hardest thing she'd ever had to do.

His reaction had been everything she had expected yet it had hurt far more than she'd imagined it would to hear him call her a 'devious little liar' and a 'cold-hearted bitch', and know that she'd deserved it. She *had* set out to deceive him. She *had* deliberately led him on, although, in her own defence, she'd simply wanted to teach him a lesson, not break his heart, and the thought was so painful all of a sudden that she rushed on.

'We just had a difference of opinion once upon a time and he hasn't forgiven me for it.'

'Funny. It's not like him to bear a grudge.' June frowned as she glanced over to where Adam was standing. 'Oh, he's a real tartar when it comes to work and won't accept anything less than a hundred and ten percent effort from his staff, but I've always found him very fair, I have to say.'

Kasey didn't say anything. There was no point trying to correct June when it would only lead to more questions. However, Adam certainly hadn't behaved fairly towards her brother. He'd made Keiran's life hell with his constant criticisms when her brother had worked for him. It had been so bad, in fact, that Keiran had given up medicine in the end and it had been the start of a downward spiral from which he was only now recovering.

'Kasey's an unusual name. How do you spell it? With a K or a C?'

Kasey was relieved to turn her thoughts to less stressful topics when Lorraine spoke to her. 'With a K. My name is actually Kathleen Christine but it caused no end of confusion when I was a child. My gran was called Kathleen, you see, and each of her sons wanted to name their first daughter after her.' She rolled her eyes. 'It wouldn't have been a problem if all four of them hadn't had a girl. At family get-togethers Gran used to shout 'Kathleen' and we'd all come running. In the end she decided it was easier to call us by the initial letters of our names so I ended up as Kasey and it just sort of stuck.'

June laughed. 'You should fit right in, then. We're really big on nicknames. You'll find a lot of the folk who work for Worlds Together have them.'

'Really? So what's Adam's nickname?' she asked, grinning.

'I don't have one.'

She spun round when she recognised the gravelly voice and felt her pulse leap when she found Adam standing behind her. It was an effort to respond with an outward show of calm when her heart was hammering but there was no way that she was letting him have the upper hand. 'Why not? Surely it's not beneath your dignity to have a nickname, Adam?'

'Not at all. I've no idea why I haven't been given one. Maybe you could suggest something?'

He had batted the ball right back into her side of the court and Kasey drummed up a laugh. 'Oh, I can think of a few which would suit you but it might be wiser to keep them to myself in the interests of team harmony.'

'How very diplomatic of you, Kasey. You're obviously on your best behaviour today because it's not like you to hold back. I got the distinct impression the last time we met that you rather enjoy causing a stir.'

'Did you? I really can't remember what happened, I'm afraid. Would you care to remind me?' she challenged. If he thought he was going to make her back down by bringing up the past, he was in for a shock.

'Oh, I don't think it would be appropriate to tell everyone, do you?' His voice dropped, the gravelly tones taking on a velvet smoothness that made the tiny hairs on the back of her neck spring to attention. 'Some things are best remembered in private, Kasey. And *that* is definitely one of them.'

He gave her a slow smile then walked away. There was a moment's stunned silence after he'd left before June let out a small gasp.

'Phew! I don't know about the rest of you but I can definitely feel a hot flush coming on!'

Everyone laughed as June fanned herself with her hand. Kasey shot her a grateful look, glad the nurse had helped to dispel the tension, but she couldn't deny that she was shaken by what had happened. She'd known that Adam wouldn't welcome her with open arms and had been prepared for his wrath, but it hadn't been anger that she'd seen in his eyes just now, had it?

A shudder ran through her as she quickly excused herself, hearing the chatter that broke out as soon as she moved away from the group. The other women had seen it too so there was no point trying to tell herself that she'd been mistaken. Adam hadn't threatened her—he hadn't needed to because he'd used a far more effective method of evening the score, one that would cause maximum damage. He'd taken the attraction they'd felt for one another five years ago and used it against her. Now all she could do was wait and see what happened. But it wasn't going to be easy, was it?

She closed her eyes as panic gripped her. Maybe she did still blame Adam for ruining her brother's life, but it hadn't stopped her wanting him before and it might not be enough to stop her wanting him again.

CHAPTER TWO

'IT's not the ideal start by any means but we'll just have to cope the best way we can.'

Adam looked around the room, hoping he'd managed to convince everyone that they shouldn't let this latest setback deter them. His gaze landed on Kasey and lingered for a moment before he forced it to move on.

It had been a mistake to use that tone with her before and he couldn't understand why he'd done it. The other women had picked up the sexual innuendo in his voice just as Kasey had done, and he hated to imagine what they must be thinking. He'd always guarded his private life, mainly because of the way he'd been brought up. As the only child of elderly parents who had discouraged any displays of emotion, he'd learned at an early age to keep his feelings to himself. It had only been when he'd met Kasey, in fact, that he'd opened up, and it was doubly galling to know that he hadn't learned from his mistakes.

'It should only be a couple of days before the bulk of our equipment arrives.' He forced himself to concentrate on the problems they faced because it was pointless worrying about the mistakes he'd made, both past and present. 'That means the theatre tents, generators, lighting equipment—things like that. We'll be able to take all our drugs, dressings and surgical instruments with us because they're within the weight restrictions so that's something, at least.'

'But where are we going to operate?' David Preston, the other surgeon on the team, put in worriedly. 'From what I've read, the hospitals over there are in an appalling state.'

'My contact in Mwuranda has promised to get one of

the theatres up and running before we arrive,' Adam assured him. 'We'll be based in Arumba which is where the main hospital is situated. The equipment there will be very basic by our standards, of course, but that won't matter too much because we'll be taking all our surgical instruments with us. I'm confident that Matthias will be able to provide us with a sterile environment to work in and that's the most important thing at the moment.'

'What about the anaesthetic equipment?' Kasey put in quietly. 'It would be helpful to have some idea what's available.'

'I'll have to check with Matthias about that and get back to you,' he replied shortly, trying to keep the edge out of his voice, then sighed when he saw the look Mary and Lorraine exchanged. Obviously he'd failed to hide his feelings again and it was worrying to know how vulnerable he was around Kasey.

The thought was like the proverbial red rag and he had to make a conscious effort not to let her see how furious he was with her for putting him in this position. She must have known how hard he would find it to work with her yet she'd still gone ahead and joined the team. It just seemed to prove all over again how little she'd ever cared about him.

'I suggest that you and Daniel work out if you'll need to make any changes to the anaesthetic agents we're taking with us.' He handed her a printed list of the drugs, trying not to let that thought do any more damage. 'You may need to order something to tide you over until our equipment arrives.'

'Looks like we'd better dig out some old textbooks,' she said lightly, smiling at Daniel, who was sitting beside her. 'I bet it's been a while since you got out the ether.'

'Too right! Still, I'm game for a bit of late-night swotting if you are, Kasey.'

Everyone laughed as Daniel leered suggestively at her. Adam stood up, shoving his hands into his pockets in case he gave in to the urge to thump the younger man on the nose. It was just the usual show of high-spirits everyone exhibited before setting off on a mission, he told himself sternly. It certainly didn't mean that Daniel was seriously going to make a play for Kasey. However, it was hard to remain calm when he watched them leave the office together a short time later and it worried him that he should feel so possessive. Kasey had played him for a fool five years ago and he really shouldn't care what she did!

'Are you sure you're up to handling this situation?'

He looked round when Shiloh approached him. 'What do you mean?'

'It's obvious there's still something going on between you and Kasey Harris so I'd understand if you decided to delay the trip until another anaesthetist can be found.'

'No.' Adam was shaking his head even before his friend had finished speaking. 'There's no way that I'm putting it off for Kasey Harris or anyone else, for that matter. I've spent months planning this visit and if we don't go now, we might not get another chance.'

'Fair enough but just go easy on yourself, eh.' Shiloh clapped him on the shoulder. 'None of us are immune when Cupid's arrow strikes. I should know because the last thing I'd intended was to fall head over heels in love when I met Rachel!'

'I'm not in love with Kasey!' Adam denied hotly.

'No? That's OK then, isn't it.'

Shiloh didn't say anything else before he left. However, Adam knew that his friend hadn't believed him. He sighed as he shut the door and sat down behind his desk because he couldn't help wondering what he was going to do. He wasn't in love with Kasey any more but he did still have feelings for her; that was obvious. He wasn't sure exactly what sort of feelings they were but he would have to be on his guard from now on. He'd be thrown off balance by seeing her today but from this point on he would think of Dr Kasey Harris as just another member of his team. And if she didn't come up to scratch, she would have to leave because he certainly wasn't doing her any favours after what she'd done to him!

He groaned because his resolve to treat her as just another member of the team had lasted the whole of ten seconds. How on earth was he going to get through the next four weeks?

Kasey was the last to arrive at Worlds Together's headquarters the following evening. Although, Shiloh had given her instructions on how to find the dockside warehouse, she must have taken a wrong turning somewhere along the way. She groaned as everyone sent up a resounding cheer when she walked into the building.

'Sorry. I've no excuse for being late. I'm just a really rotten map reader!'

'So long as you made it in the end,' June said cheerfully. 'Anyway, you've not missed much. Adam was just running through the rosters although they'll probably change in a couple of days' time. Once the heat's on, everyone just mucks in and gets the job done.'

'Fine by me,' Kasey agreed, sitting down on a packing case. She glanced at Adam and raised her brows when he gave her a cold stare. She'd made up her mind last night that no matter what he said or did, she wasn't going to react. Cool and professional seemed the best method of approach so she would stick to that.

'Over to you then, Adam,' she said sweetly.

'As I was saying, we'll work the usual twelve-hour shifts to start with. The important thing to remember is that we have to pace ourselves. I don't want any heroics and people trying to prove they can do the job better than anyone else because it will cause more problems than it will solve. We need good, steady work and that's all.'

He ignored her as he looked around the assembled group but she could tell from his tone that his remarks had been aimed at her. After all, she was the only one without any experience of working in the field so he didn't need to remind the others about what was required of them. Her temper moved a notch up the scale although she forbore to say anything. If Adam was trying to provoke a reaction, he'd have to try harder than that.

'I'm afraid that conditions are worse than I thought. My contact, Matthias, managed to get a message to me last night to warn me that there are several rebel groups still active in the area where we'll be based. The Mwurandan government is doing everything it can to restore order but there's no guarantee they'll have the situation under control by the time we arrive.'

Once again his gaze swept over them and once again he ignored her. Kasey's temper moved another notch up the scale.

'This mission is going to be both difficult and dangerous,' he concluded. 'So if anyone wishes to back out, now is the time to do so.'

This time his gaze landed squarely on her and her spine stiffened when she saw the challenge in his eyes. It was obvious that he didn't believe she was up to the job and it stung to know what a poor opinion he had of her.

'If that was directed at me, Adam, then I hate to disappoint you. You're not getting rid of me that easily.'

'It wasn't directed specifically at anyone. I just want to be sure that everyone understands the problems we will have to face.'

She flushed when she heard the dismissive note in his voice. She knew that he'd used it deliberately to cut her down to size and didn't need the sympathetic smile June gave her to prove that. The meeting broke up shortly afterwards but she knew that she had to sort out the situation soon. It would be hard enough to cope with the pressures of the job without having Adam getting at her all the time. When he left the main part of the warehouse, she followed him.

'We need to talk—'

'I haven't time to soothe your injured feelings,' he said shortly, striding into the office. 'If you don't like the way I treated you then you know what to do.'

'And that's what you want, is it? You want me to leave?'

'Frankly, I don't give a damn what you do, Kasey. What I won't put up with is you expecting special treatment.' He sat down behind the overflowing desk and picked up a bundle of papers. 'You're just another member of the team as far as I'm concerned so don't go getting it into your head that I'm singling you out.'

'Rubbish! You wouldn't have spoken that way to any of the others.' Her anger rocketed the rest of the way up the scale and she glared at him. 'You don't want me on this team because of what happened five years ago so don't try telling me that you aren't singling me out when it's blatantly obvious that's exactly what you are doing. You haven't forgiven me for what I did to you, have you, Adam? You can't accept that I got the better of you!'

'You're wrong. I accepted it at the same time I accepted what a fool I'd been to think I was in love with you.' His eyes grazed over her, filled with such contempt that her heart trembled with sudden pain. 'The truth is that I was never in love with you, Kasey. The woman I loved was an illusion, someone you conjured up to pay me back for what you mistakenly believed I'd done to your brother. And that Kasey Harris doesn't exist.'

He pushed back his chair and stood up. Kasey didn't move as he brushed past her. She couldn't because movement demanded too much effort. What Adam had accused her of doing was true. She had set out to make him fall for her because of what he'd done to Keiran. What he was wrong about was that she'd taken on a different persona or, as he'd put it, conjured up a different Kasey Harris. She hadn't needed to do that because from the moment they'd met she had responded to him instinctively.

A sob welled to her lips but she bit it back because there was no point crying now. It wouldn't help and certainly wouldn't change what had happened. The truth was that the Kasey Harris he'd fallen in love with had been her real self; the woman who had broken his heart had been the myth, the person she'd created. And what made it all so much worse was that Adam would never believe her if she told him that.

'Not exactly the Hilton, is it?'

'Oh, I don't know. It has a certain exotic charm,' Kasey replied in response to June's quip.

They'd just arrived at the hostel where they would be living during their stay in Mwuranda after a long and tiring journey. Their plane had turned out to be an old cargo aircraft, chartered by the Red Cross to deliver a consignment of food and clothing to the country. Make-shift seats had been squeezed into the hold between the packing cases so the noise of the engines had been deafening. After all those hours spent in such noisy and cramped surroundings anywhere looked good.

'Exotic is right.' June swatted a massive cockroach off the chest of drawers and shuddered. 'You don't get wild-life this big in Surbiton!'

'Look on the bright side,' Kasey said, chuckling. 'Once

you've dealt with one of these little suckers, your average British beetle is child's play!'

She looked round when Lorraine and Mary suddenly appeared. There were four beds in the room and they'd obviously decided to join them. 'Welcome to the bridal suite,' she declared in her most unctuous tone. 'We hope your stay here will be everything you expect it to be.'

'Sadly, that will probably turn out to be the case,' Lorraine said pithily, looking round. 'What a dump. It's a good job my Tim didn't book us into somewhere like this for our honeymoon or it would have been the shortest marriage on record!'

'You mean you don't like it?' Kasey looked affronted as she swept the cover off one of the narrow single beds. 'No expense has been spared to provide us with the ultimate in comfort. I mean, just inhale that aroma. Eau de mildew if I'm not mistaken.'

'You were warned about the conditions before you came, Dr Harris, so I hope you aren't going to bombard us with an on-going litany of complaints.'

Kasey swung round when she heard Adam's voice coming from the doorway. She hadn't spoken to him to since he'd walked out of the office the previous night. He'd been sitting near the front of the plane when she'd boarded it so she'd deliberately chosen a seat at the rear to avoid him. However, his attitude towards her obviously hadn't softened during the journey, she realised when she saw the chill in his eyes.

'I wasn't complaining, Dr Chandler. I was merely making an observation. I assume it isn't against the rules to voice an opinion?'

'Not so long as it doesn't create unrest within the team.' He stared back at her, unwilling to give an inch let alone concede that he might possibly be over-reacting. 'Team harmony is essential and I shall come down extremely hard on anyone who undermines it.'

He didn't add anything else before he went on his way but he'd said more than enough by that point. June grimaced.

'Someone seems to have left his sense of humour at home. Try not to let it get to you, Kasey. His bark really is worse than his bite.'

'I'm not sure if I want to test out that theory,' she replied lightly, not wanting the others to know how much it had hurt to be spoken to in that fashion. The fact that it had been so unjust to reprimand her was what really rankled but there was little she could do about it. If she caused a fuss then Adam would accuse her of disrupting the team and use it as an excuse to send her back to England.

Well, if that was what he was hoping for, he was going to be disappointed, she decided, stiffening her spine. She could put up with anything he cared to dish out!

They unpacked their bags then June checked her watch. 'It's only four o'clock so how about a tour of the building before dinner to get our bearings?'

'Good idea,' Kasey agreed immediately although the other two shook their heads.

'I'm bushed,' Mary exclaimed, sinking down onto one of the beds. 'I need a bit of shut-eye if I'm to be the life and soul of the party this evening.'

'What party?' Kasey asked in surprise.

'Oh, it's a bit of a tradition with Adam. He always has a get-together on our first night,' Lorraine explained. 'He sees it as a way for us all to bond. Anyhow, I think I'll follow Mary's example and test out the bed springs while you two intrepid souls go exploring. Have fun.'

'We'll do our best,' Kasey replied, following June out of the room.

They made their way along the corridor, peering into

the rooms they passed. They'd been told that the hostel had been used by students from the local college before the rebel uprising and the facilities were very basic. All the bedrooms were fitted out exactly like their room with four single beds and a chest of drawers. There was no carpet on any of the floors but the worn brown linoleum had been swept clean. There was also a small bathroom at the end of the corridor with a lavatory next to it and she heaved a sigh of relief.

'At least we have indoor plumbing. I had visions of having to creep out of the building in the middle of the night to go to the loo.'

'All mod cons by the look of it,' June declared, flushing the toilet.

They made their way up the stairs to the floor above which was exactly the same: bedrooms with a bathroom and a lavatory at the end of the corridor. Although everywhere smelled a little musty, it was obvious that attempts had been made to clean the place in readiness for their arrival.

'It's better than I expected,' Kasey admitted as they went down to the ground floor where a large square entrance hall led to a sitting room on one side and a dining room on the other with the kitchen and storerooms beyond that.

'It is. I had no idea what to expect when Adam told me where we would be staying.' June shrugged when she looked at her in surprise. 'Although I've been on a lot of missions, I've never been to an area like this before where they've only recently stopped fighting so I wasn't sure how bad the facilities would be.'

'I see. That makes me feel a bit better. I thought I was the only one who didn't have any experience and you were all old hands at this game,' she confessed wryly.

'Not at all. OK, so most of us have worked overseas

and you haven't but working in a war zone will be a whole new experience for all of us except Adam, of course. He's already done a stint here.'

'Really?' Kasey stopped and stared at her. 'Adam's worked here before?'

'Yes. Didn't you know? He spent a year in Mwuranda with a French aid team but they pulled out when the fighting started. Adam decided to stay on and he only came back to England because he was injured, quite badly, too, I believe, although he never talks about it.' June sighed. 'I always thought there was more to it than just a desire to help which kept him here. It was almost as though he didn't care about his own safety.'

'When did this all happen?' she asked slowly, feeling a cold chill envelop her.

'I'm not sure...four, five years ago. Something like that.'

Which would be shortly after she'd told him how she'd tricked him, she realised sickly. Had that been the reason why Adam had shown such disregard for his own safety..because he'd been so upset by what she'd done that he'd no longer cared what had happened to him? She didn't want to believe it but the timing pointed towards it being true. Frankly, she didn't know how it made her feel to know that he'd put his life in danger because of her actions, but it did make her see how difficult it would be to resolve their differences.

She frowned. Was that what she really wanted, though? Initially, all she'd hoped to do was draw a line under the past but, strangely, it no longer seemed enough. She'd never been someone who enjoyed being at odds with other people; it simply wasn't in her nature. Maybe that was why she'd found it so difficult to put the whole unhappy episode behind her. It had played constantly on her mind so maybe it was time to try and end the hostilities between them, although it wouldn't be easy, of course.

Her heart suddenly sank because the thought that she might never be able to make her peace with him was very hard to bear, for some reason.

Dinner that night turned out to be quite a convivial affair. The catering team did them proud, serving up a meal which would have put many high-class restaurants to shame. Kasey found it a little daunting at first to be thrown in at the deep end and expected to mingle. Everyone else had worked together at some point and she couldn't help feeling like the outsider. Although she knew that she could tag along with June and the other nurses, she didn't want to get in the way when they were obviously eager to catch up with what their friends had been doing.

In the end it was Daniel who saved the day. He took it upon himself to introduce her to everyone present and soon put her at her ease as he filled her in on people's backgrounds. He also insisted she sit with him at dinner and regaled her with stories of other missions he'd been on so that by the end of the evening Kasey felt more like one of the team. The only disquieting note throughout the whole evening, in fact, was that Adam ignored her. He spoke to everyone else present but made no attempt to speak to her. It was as though she didn't exist and she had to admit that it hurt to be treated in such an off-hand fashion.

The party finally broke up around midnight. Everyone was worn out after the journey and started to drift away. Daniel begged her to stay and have a final cup of coffee with him but she refused first of all because she was tired and secondly because she didn't want him getting the wrong idea. She liked Daniel but there was no way that she was going to risk inciting Adam's wrath by getting romantically involved with him or anyone else.

She bade Daniel a studiedly casual goodnight and made her way across the hall. Most people had gone straight up to bed so there was nobody about. She headed towards the stairs then paused as she passed the front door. Even though she was bone-tired as well, she desperately needed a breath of fresh air before turning in for the night.

She let herself out of the hostel and walked down the path, carefully picking her way through the rubble. Like most of the buildings they'd passed on the drive from the airfield, the hostel had suffered extensive damage during the recent fighting. Kasey stopped when she reached a clump of straggly bushes and looked back at the building, trying to imagine what it must have been like for the students who'd lived there during those troubled times. It must have been awful for them, living in constant danger—

The sharp report of a rifle cracked through the still night air and she jumped. She spun round to see where the shot had come from then gasped in alarm when a figure suddenly materialised out of the shadows and hurled her to the ground.

'Let me go,' she screamed, punching the man's broad back with her clenched fists. 'Let…me…go, damn you!'

'For God's sake, woman!' Adam's face suddenly loomed into view and she gulped when she realised that he was her attacker.

'What the hell do you think you're doing?' she snapped, glaring up at him.

'Saving your damned life.' He put his hand over her mouth when she went to speak. 'Just shut up, Kasey. There's someone out there shooting at us so this is neither the time nor the place to discuss your injured feelings.'

Kasey fell silent, not that she could have said very much with his hand clamped over her mouth. She could feel the hard pressure of his fingers on her lips and a tingle of awareness that was totally inappropriate for the seriousness of the situation scudded through her. All of a sudden she became alarmingly aware of the intimacy of their position. Adam was lying right on top of her, his broad chest squashing her breasts, his hips and thighs crushing her against the rocky ground. Every muscle in his body was rigid with tension as he drew back his head and looked around the clearing, and a small moan rushed up her throat because she could feel every single one of them.

Intimately.

Trapezius, pectoralis major, deltoid, obliquuos externus... She made herself recite the names of all those muscles from memory, hoping it would help if she focused on some basic anatomy rather than the effect they were having on her. It worked to a point until another volley of shots suddenly cracked through the air. Yelping in fear, she buried her face in his chest and wrapped her arms around him. He felt so big and solid that she clung fast, using him as her rock in an unstable world.

'It's OK.' His hand strayed from her mouth and her heart leapt again when she felt his fingers gently stroking her hair. 'They're not firing at us. Whoever they're aiming at is in those trees over to our left.'

His voice rumbled up from his chest and she shuddered when she felt its vibrations rippling into her. Adam obviously misunderstood her reaction because his tone deepened, taking on the soothing cadence people use with the very scared.

'They probably don't even know we're here, Kasey, so all we need to do is sit tight until it's over. OK?'

'OK,' she muttered in mortification, because if she'd hoped to impress him with her sang-froid under fire she'd obviously failed.

They stayed where they were for another ten minutes, although it felt a lot longer than that to her. It wasn't just the fact that Adam was squashing her with his weight that bothered her so much, but that she was enjoying the experience. She should have loathed this kind of intimate contact with him but although her mind knew that, her body didn't. Every time he shifted his weight, she had to make a conscious effort not to respond so that it was a relief when he finally decided the danger had passed.

'Stay there while I check out the lie of the land,' he instructed tersely, easing himself away from her. He cautiously stood up, keeping well back into the shadows as he looked around for the gunman.

'He seems to have gone,' he said at last, glancing down at her. 'Let's get back inside but keep your head down and stay close to the bushes just in case.'

Kasey scrambled to her feet and brushed the grit off her backside, wincing when her fingers encountered a dozen different sore spots caused by being squashed on the stony ground. Adam took another quick look around then pointed towards the path, silently indicating that she should go ahead of him.

They'd almost reached the front doors of the hostel when a man suddenly appeared from around the side of the building. Kasey didn't have time to react as Adam grabbed hold of her and thrust her behind him, using himself as a shield in case the man had a gun, but even as they watched, the stranger dropped to his knees then slumped face down onto the ground.

'Looks like he's the guy who was being shot at,' Adam shouted as he ran forward. Kasey raced after him, dropping to her knees and staring in horror at the gaping wound in the back of the young man's right shoulder.

'He's been hit, and more than once, by the look of it.' Adam pointed to the twin exit wounds caused when the bullets had torn through the flesh. 'I'm not sure how many bullets were fired so there might be others still inside him.

I'll have to check. There's bound to be extensive soft tissue damage, though, and possibly some damage to the shoulder joint so it's going to take some time to sort it all out.'

'You're going to operate?' she exclaimed.

'Of course.' He frowned. 'Although I'm not sure where would be the best place to use. One of the bedrooms would be easiest but the lighting is too poor for this kind of intricate surgery.'

'You mean that you're going to operate *here*?'

'Yes. It's far too risky to take him to the hospital. Matthias warned me that we mustn't drive around at night so we'll have to make do with whatever facilities we have here and simply hope for the best.'

'I see,' she murmured, trying to get her head round what was going on. Obviously Adam was less concerned about the injured man being a terrorist than he was about saving his life, so she made herself focus on the problem of finding a suitable place to use as a makeshift operating theatre. It would need to be somewhere with decent lighting, as he'd pointed out, and it would also help if they had access to water for washing.

'How about the dining room?' she suggested. 'The lighting isn't too bad in there and we have direct access to the kitchen. We can use one of the tables as a temporary operating table, too.'

'Good choice. Can you get everything set up while I bring him inside? I just need to stop this bleeding before I move him.'

'Here.' She quickly unbuttoned her blouse and handed it to him, thankful that she'd decided to wear a T-shirt underneath and was still decently covered up.

Adam chuckled as he took it from her and bound it tightly over the wound in the man's shoulder. 'It should have been a petticoat, by rights, of course.'

'Like in all those old western movies? Every time someone got shot, the heroine would start ripping up her petticoat for bandages. Unfortunately, it's not quite what the modern woman wears,' she told him pithily, and he laughed out loud.

'Sadly not. Jeans and a T-shirt seem to fit the bill nowadays for most occasions.' He smiled up at her, his green eyes sparkling with laughter, and her breath caught because the change it brought to his expression was enough to make her heart race. 'Still, some women manage to look good no matter what they wear.'

Kasey wasn't sure if the compliment had been aimed specifically at her or if it had been a general observation, and didn't allow herself to speculate. There really wasn't time to think about it right then, despite how tempting it was. She made her way back inside the hostel where she was greeted with relief by the rest of the team, who'd heard the commotion and had gathered in the hall.

She quickly explained what had happened, carefully omitting any mention of how Adam had tried to protect her after that first gunshot. However, she saw the speculation on several people's faces when they realised that she and Adam had both been outside when the shooting had started and knew they were putting their own interpretation on the facts.

Kasey didn't attempt to correct them—she knew it would probably make matters worse if she tried to explain that they hadn't arranged to meet in the grounds of the hostel—but it was unsettling to know that she and Adam were being linked together like this. It was an added pressure she could have done without but, fortunately, there was too much to do to worry about it. As soon as she'd sorted out some volunteers to help, she headed for the kitchen to get everything ready.

'We'll use one of the tables,' she instructed, pointing to

the largest of the refectory tables. 'If you can move it directly under the central light fitting, that would be best.'

Daniel and Alan Jones, their radiographer, immediately set to and moved the heavy table into position while she and June went to find some theatre drapes and dressings. Their equipment had been piled into one of the empty storerooms off the kitchen and it didn't take them long to sort out what they needed. Kasey also collected a set of sterile surgical instruments, although she didn't break open the pack but just placed it on a nearby table. Adam could open it once he was ready to operate.

'Everything sorted?'

Adam came into the room with the injured man draped over his shoulders. Daniel and Alan helped him lie the man on the table then he looked round. 'Right. I don't need all of you here so I'll just take a couple of volunteers. June will you do the honours? And, Daniel if you could cover the anaesthetic?'

'Excuse me?' Kasey stepped forward, barely able to contain her annoyance at the way he had deliberately cut her out of the proceedings. 'There's no need to involve Daniel. I'm perfectly capable of handling this.'

'You had a shock tonight,' he replied curtly, walking into the kitchen and turning on the old-fashioned, hot-water geyser. 'I suggest you get a good night's sleep and give yourself time to get over it.'

'Was that a suggestion or an order?' she demanded, following him into the room.

'It's simple common sense.' He pumped a handful of antiseptic solution out of the dispenser she'd placed there for them to use and lathered his forearms.

'In that case, wouldn't it be sensible if you excused yourself as well?' She stared back at him, experiencing a pang of regret when she saw the flicker of annoyance that had lit his green eyes. There was no sign of amusement in them now. 'You were shot at, too, Adam, don't forget, so you had just as big a shock as me. If I'm not up to handling this job, neither are you.'

'I shall decide whether or not I'm fit to operate.'

'And I shall decide whether or not I'm fit to act as your anaesthetist.'

She stared back at him, knowing that if she lost this battle it wouldn't be worth her staying on in Mwuranda. If he didn't trust her to do her job then she would have to go home. Maybe she could put up with his hostility on a personal level but she refused to compromise when it came to her work.

'Fair enough.'

He inclined his head in brief acknowledgement then spun round on his heel. Kasey let out her breath in a small sigh of relief, only then acknowledging how important it was to her that she should be allowed to stay. She quickly scrubbed up and put on a gown then went back to the kitchen. June had set up a drip and was now cleaning the injured man's shoulder with antiseptic solution. The rest of the team had gone back to bed, so all she could hope was that Adam's apparent lack of faith in her hadn't caused any long-term damage. It would be difficult to work with the other members of the team if they had doubts about her ability.

It was a sobering thought and it put her on her mettle as she began anaesthetising the patient. Without the aid of artificial ventilation equipment, she couldn't administer a muscle relaxant otherwise the patient wouldn't be able to breathe, so she opted for an anaesthetic agent and pain relief, administering the drugs via a cannula in the back of the man's hand because it would be easy to top up the drugs throughout the operation.

The lack of modern equipment also meant that she would have to rely more heavily on physical signs to en-

sure the patient was maintained at a suitable level of un-
consciousness. Increased sweating and salivation, irregular
breathing, changes in muscle tone and eye movement were
all indications that a patient was receiving an inadequate
level of anaesthesia. She would also need to monitor his
general status through his heart rate and blood pressure, so
she would be kept busy, but she had no doubts about her
ability to do the job. She was a first-rate anaesthetist and
she intended to prove that to Adam and everyone else on
the team.

'I'll just get this mess tidied up first.'

Adam snapped on a second pair of gloves as he came
over to the table. They were all wearing a double layer of
gloves because they'd been warned about the dangers of
HIV. He quickly debrided the torn flesh surrounding the
exit wounds then removed some splinters of bone that had
sheared off from the shoulder joint. He delicately probed
the trajectory the bullets had taken with his finger and
shook his head.

'No sign of any more bullets lodged in there, I'm
pleased to say.'

Kasey nodded, not wanting anything to distract her as
she checked the patient's BP. It was a little on the low
side, which wasn't unusual considering the amount of
blood he'd lost, but she still reported her findings.

'BP's a bit low. I'll increase the drip.'

'Fine.' Adam barely glanced at her as he began the delicate task of repairing the torn shoulder muscle. He shook
his head. 'There's a tear right through the deltoid. It's going to need a lot of physio to get this arm moving properly
again.'

Once again Kasey didn't say anything. She was too busy
checking her patient. His skin was dry to the touch and
there was no sign of an increase in his temperature, which
were both good signs.

'How's he doing so far?'

She looked up when Adam spoke to her, feeling her tension lessen just a little when she saw no sign of concern in the green eyes that were watching her over the top of his face mask. 'He's stable at the moment. BP has levelled out and his temperature is normal. Pulse rate and breathing are both within acceptable levels.'

'Good.'

He gave her the ghost of a smile, only visible by the slight lifting at the corners of his eyes, and she huffed out a tiny sigh of relief at having passed muster. June handed him a scalpel then winked at her, and Kasey chuckled. June had obviously noted the small improvement in his attitude towards her so all she could do now was hope that it would last.

They carried on in surprising harmony after that until Adam nodded. 'That's about all I can do for now. I'll just pack the wound and leave it open to drain. Infection is always a major problem with this type of injury because the bullet carries all sorts of gunk into the body, but we'll just have to deal with it as and when it happens. There might be other damage, of course. A high-velocity gunshot injury causes shock waves to pass through the body but we'll have to wait for the X-rays before we can know for certain what's happened.'

'Will you do the X-rays here or at the hospital?' Kasey asked.

'Hospital. We'll have him moved over there tomorrow if he's fit enough to withstand the journey.'

Adam slid a drainage tube into the wound, packed it with layers of gauze then covered it with a light dressing before they rolled the patient onto his side so he could dress the entry wounds, which were far smaller—no bigger than a couple of ten-pence pieces.

'It might be best if we kept him sedated tonight,' he told

her when he'd finished. 'We have no idea who he is and I don't want to take the chance of him wandering around during the night.'

'I'll sort it out,' she assured him as June went to fetch some more dressings from the storeroom. 'And I'll stay with him, of course, to make sure there isn't a problem.'

'There's no need. I'll do it myself.'

He turned away but if he thought she was letting him get away with that, he could think again. She grabbed hold of his arm, her blue eyes filled with a mixture of pain and injured pride as she stared into his face.

'What is it with you, Adam? Do you get a thrill out of undermining me all the time? Or are you hoping that I'll crack if you keep on pushing me? I know I hurt you—'

'It has nothing to do with what happened between us,' he said curtly, shrugging off her hand.

'No?' She laughed scornfully. 'Come on, Adam, at least have the guts to tell me the truth. We both know that you didn't want me along on this trip and we both know why, too.'

'And that has nothing whatsoever to do with my decision to take charge of this patient tonight.'

He brushed past her, his face like thunder as he stripped off his gloves and tossed them into the waste sack. Kasey followed him into the kitchen, too incensed to care if she was making matters worse. Maybe she should accept his decision, but how could she when it seemed to be yet another deliberate slight?

'Then what does it have to do with? I think I deserve an answer, Adam.'

'I don't have to give you an answer.' He gripped hold of the sink and she could tell that he was struggling to keep a rein on his temper. 'I'm in charge of this team and it's up to me what happens.'

'I should have known you'd take the easy way out,' she

scoffed. 'You're very good at finding fault with people but you're not so good when it comes to backing it up with cold, hard facts.'

'I am *not* finding fault with you or your work!'

'Then why won't you leave me in charge of this patient?'

'Because it's too bloody dangerous, that's why!'

He swung round and she took a step back when she saw the anger in his eyes yet she knew on some inner level that it wasn't directed at her but at himself. Her heart began to pound so that it was difficult to hear what he was saying as he continued in the same biting tone.

'I am simply not prepared to put your life at risk, Kasey. And if you don't like it then there isn't much I can do because nothing you say or do will make me change my mind.'

'I didn't realise…'

She stopped and swallowed because she couldn't seem to find the right words to explain that she'd never expected him to be concerned about her safety. It seemed too incredible to believe after what had gone on between them, yet there wasn't a doubt in her mind that he was telling her the truth.

'If you could just make sure that he'll be unconscious for the rest of the night that will be fine.' His tone was less abrasive now, softer, and she took a deep breath as her anger suddenly melted away leaving her feeling incredibly vulnerable.

'Of course,' she murmured, turning to hurry back into the dining room before he realised how shaken she felt.

Adam followed her and her heart ached when she glanced up and saw him standing at the end of the table. He looked so tired and drawn, his skin tinged with the grey hue of fatigue, that all of a sudden she felt her eyes welling with tears. It was her presence that had caused him to look like this and it wasn't what she'd intended. She'd come on this trip first and foremost to make the lives of the people they treated that bit better, not to make *his* life more stressful.

'I'm sorry,' she whispered, overwhelmed by guilt.

'Because you stood up for yourself?' He shrugged. 'I'd have done the same thing, Kasey, so there's no need to apologise.'

'I'm sorry for making things difficult for you,' she corrected, wanting—*needing*—to explain. 'I never meant to do that.'

'Didn't you?' His voice sounded flat, emotionless, and she sighed, understanding why he found it so hard to believe her.

'No,' she said briefly, because there was no point trying to convince him when he didn't want to be convinced. She topped up the patient's anaesthetic then checked his vital signs one last time and stepped away from the table.

'He should be OK now but you can top up the anaesthetic if you need to. I've left everything ready for you.' She pointed to the vials of drugs then made her way to the door. 'Goodnight.'

'Goodnight, Kasey. And thank you.'

She didn't pause, didn't turn back to ask him what exactly he was thanking her for, because she knew what his answer would be and that it wasn't the one she really wanted to hear. Adam was thanking her for her work that night, for acting as his anaesthetist and doing her job well. Every surgeon she'd ever worked with had done that because it was what was expected of one professional to another. However, as she made her way upstairs, she couldn't help wishing that Adam's thanks had been a bit more personal, that he'd thanked her for being *her*, not just a colleague.

It made her see just how ambivalent her feelings were

towards him, and how hard it was going to be to work with him because of that. She might be ready to fight tooth and nail to uphold her status within the team but it didn't mean that she didn't want Adam's approval, did it?

All of a sudden it felt as though she'd come full circle and was back to where she'd been five years ago, when wanting and hating Adam had almost destroyed her. Would she survive this time?

CHAPTER THREE

'START her off with two litres of saline but I want it pushed through as quickly as possible.'

Adam was hard-pressed to contain his anger as he looked at the young girl lying on the bed. Amelia Undobe had been celebrating her thirteenth birthday that day when she'd stepped on a land-mine close to her home. Her right foot had been blown off in the explosion and the left one had suffered such extensive damage that he wasn't sure if he'd be able to save it. It was hard to suppress his fury when he saw what had been done to the child, but he couldn't allow his emotions to get the better of him or he wouldn't be able to do his job properly. He turned to June and there was no trace of what he was feeling as he continued.

'She's too dehydrated to undergo surgery at the moment so we need to get her fluid levels up. I'll be back in a few minutes to take another look at her so do what you can.'

He stripped off his gloves and tossed them into the waste sack then left the treatment room. Every muscle in his body was aching with tiredness and it was his own fault, too. Hadn't he laid down the law about people not trying to prove themselves? So why was he pushing himself to the point of exhaustion? Did he really think it would stop him thinking about Kasey if he worked until he dropped? He'd still be thinking about her on his deathbed at this rate, still feeling this same mixture of longing and anguish that was eating away at him, and he sighed wearily as he headed along the corridor because he knew what had set it off.

Feeling her lying beneath him the other night had awoken urges he'd thought he'd conquered years ago. He might have been trying to protect her but his body had taken a completely different view of what had been happening and he'd been paying the penalty ever since. For the past three nights he'd dreamt about her—felt her softness over and over again, smelled the perfume of her skin—and now the images seemed to be locked inside his head and he couldn't seem to shift them no matter how hard he tried. The thought of having to put up with such misery for an unknown period of time was more than he could bear and he cursed roundly as he veered off towards the canteen. Maybe a cup of coffee would give him the boost he needed and set him back on track.

'Ah, Adam, my friend. I was just coming to find you.'

'That sounds ominous.'

Adam drummed up a smile when Matthias caught up with him. He'd met Matthias when he'd been working with the French aid team during his first visit to the country and they had remained friends ever since. Matthias had qualified as a doctor in England but he'd returned to Mwuranda after completing his training and worked in the hospital they were currently using as their base. Adam knew that Matthias could have left when so many other educated people had fled the country but he'd stayed and done all he could to help his people during the war. It was because of Matthias that he'd agreed to run this mission, in fact.

'So what's gone wrong this time?' he demanded as Matthias fell into step with him.

'How do you know it's bad news?'

Matthias smiled at him, his teeth gleaming against his black skin. A tall, handsome man in his thirties, he had the looks and the bearing to have achieved great things in the world of medicine. It was a measure of his character that he'd turned his back on material success to help his countrymen.

'Instinct? A lucky guess?' Adam replied drolly, shouldering his way into the canteen. Although the catering team had done their best, the place still bore the evidence of the recent turmoil—the walls were riddled with bullet holes and most of the glass was missing from the windows. Still, the coffee was hot and strong so that was something to be grateful for.

He went over to the urn and filled a couple of mugs with the steaming black brew then carried them over to a table. There were a few other people taking a break as well, and he averted his eyes when he spotted Kasey and Daniel sitting at a table in the corner. Hooking out a chair with his foot, he sat down and shoved one of the mugs across the table.

'You are far too cynical, my friend,' Matthias reproached him. 'It does no good to expect bad things to happen all the time. What is the point of always expecting the worst?'

'That way you don't risk being disappointed,' he replied shortly, his eyes skittering across the room before he could stop them. His mouth thinned when he saw Daniel lean over and pluck something out of Kasey's hair. It was a gesture that positively reeked of intimacy and he couldn't help glowering at the couple. To his mind, they were getting far too familiar and he would have to have a word with them—remind them that they weren't there for fun but had a job to do.

'Something has upset you, Adam?'

'What?' His gaze swivelled round when Matthias interrupted his thoughts.

'The way you were glaring at that young couple, I assumed they must have done something to upset you.'

Matthias's tone was bland but the look he gave him was far too knowing for Adam's liking.

'I prefer it if members of my team don't fraternise during working hours,' he said shortly, knowing that he sounded like a leftover from the Victorian era.

'Ah, I see. It's important to have clear guidelines so everyone understands what is expected of them, although it must be difficult for you to ensure that people stay within the accepted limits.'

Adam scowled when he heard the amusement in his friend's voice. 'I came here to do a job, not win a popularity contest, if that's what you mean. If the members of this team won't abide by my rules then they will be sent back to England.'

'But all Daniel was doing was removing a piece of lint from Dr Harris's hair. Hardly a major crime, I would have thought.' Matthias smiled faintly. 'You seem a little… sensitive where that young woman is concerned. It isn't the first time I've noticed you glaring at her.'

'Maybe I've had good reason,' he replied tersely because he hadn't realised that he'd made his feelings quite so obvious. 'Anyway, what did you want to speak to me about?' he added, swiftly changing the subject because he didn't want to talk about Kasey or his feelings for her—whatever they were. Telling her that he'd been concerned about her safety the other night was something else that had been playing on his mind. He'd tried telling himself that he would have been equally concerned for any member of the team but even he wasn't convinced it was true.

The thought did little to improve his already fragile temper and he glowered at the other man. 'Don't tell me we have another problem on our hands.'

'No. Despite what you may have thought, it's good news this time.' Thankfully, Matthias took the hint and didn't pursue the subject. 'I have just received a message to say that your equipment has arrived. It's being unloaded at this very moment, in fact, so I shall send a truck to the airfield to collect it. It would be helpful if the driver had a list so he can check that it's all there.'

'I can let you have a copy of the inventory,' Adam offered immediately. 'The last thing we want is for half of it to go missing. There's a lot of valuable equipment in that consignment.'

'Indeed.' Matthias drank some of his coffee and shuddered. Picking up a handful of sugar packets, he tore them open and tipped the contents into his mug.

Adam chuckled. 'I see you still have a sweet tooth. Remember those Belgian chocolates one of the French guys brought with him?'

'Do I?' Matthias groaned. 'I still dream about those chocolates, my friend. Their richness, the smoothness of the chocolate as it melted on one's tongue… I tell you, eating them was a truly orgasmic experience.'

'I'm sure your wife would appreciate hearing you say that,' he said dryly.

'Ah, but Sarah knows how much I love her.' Matthias laughed softly. 'She wouldn't mind me finding pleasure elsewhere so long as it was only with a box of chocolates. Passion is something we should all enjoy, no matter what form it takes.'

'I'm afraid I can't agree with you there. In my experience, passion is the most dangerous emotion of all because it makes fools of us all.'

Unbidden, his eyes skimmed across the room again and his heart contracted when he saw Kasey laughing at something Daniel had said to her. He'd never experienced real passion until he'd met her, never known what it was like to physically ache for a woman. Every time he'd been with her his heart had leapt, his breathing had grown shallow, his brain had gone fuzzy. He'd barely been able to function while he'd been in her thrall and yet at the same time he'd felt more alive than he'd felt either before or since. The passion he'd felt for Kasey had consumed him utterly, so that he'd felt like a shell when she'd left him, and the memory was more than he could stand. Pushing back his chair, he strode across the room.

'I hate to interrupt your little tête-à-tête but we're here to work, not fool around. Why are you both in here? I thought David was operating this morning so one of you should be in Theatre and the other should be assessing patients ready for the afternoon list.'

'The cleaners are in Theatre, sorting everything out after our last stint,' Daniel explained, looking somewhat taken aback. 'I thought I'd take a break while I had the chance.'

'And I felt like a cup of coffee, although I didn't realise that I needed to ask your permission first, Adam. Perhaps you'd be kind enough to give it to me retrospectively.'

Kasey stared up at him, the chill in her deep blue eyes such a contrast to the warmth he'd seen in them when she'd been talking to Daniel that his anger soared to new heights. He glared back at her, bending so that their faces were mere inches apart.

'Coffee-breaks are normally taken *after* all the work is done.'

'Which is why I'm taking my break now.' She didn't back down but held his gaze. 'I've seen everyone who's scheduled for Theatre today. If you don't believe me, you can check.'

'Including Amelia Undobe?'

'No.' Her lids flickered down for a moment before she looked at him again. 'Obviously, I made a mistake and missed her out. I apologise. I'll get right onto it.'

She pushed back her chair and stood up. Adam stepped back as she brushed past him, curbing the sudden urge he felt to call her back and apologise. He knew that he'd had no right to speak to her like that when she hadn't known that Amelia had been brought into the hospital, and was suddenly filled with self-loathing for the way he was behaving. He would have to try and make amends somehow so when Daniel stood up as well, he turned to him and shrugged.

'Sorry. I was out of order for saying that.'

'You were.' Daniel's normally cheerful expression was subdued now. 'I'm not so bothered for myself but it really isn't on to have a go at Kasey. She certainly isn't a shirker when it comes to work. In fact, she volunteered to work last night when we had an emergency rushed in, *and* turned up bang on time this morning to do her own shift.'

'I had no idea—' Adam began.

'No. I didn't think you had. You're too busy finding fault to realise what a first-rate worker she is.' Daniel pushed his chair under the table. 'And for your information, I was the one who suggested she take a coffee-break. So if you want to come down heavy on anyone, it should be me.'

'I'm sorry,' Adam repeated, but the damage had been done. Daniel was right, too, because it had been grossly unfair of him to lay into Kasey like that. There was no excuse and he certainly couldn't absolve himself by admitting that it had been seeing them together that had made him behave that way. He had no right to be jealous because Kasey enjoyed Daniel's company, no right to be jealous if she enjoyed more than that, in fact.

The thought of what that 'more' might entail was too difficult to deal with. Adam swung round and headed for the door. He needed to concentrate on work instead of letting all these other issues distract him.

'Don't forget that inventory, Adam. You were going to let me have a copy.'

Matthias followed him from the canteen and he stopped.

'Yes, of course. Sorry. It's in the office. I'll fetch it for you,' he said shortly because it wasn't like him to forget something as important as that. It just seemed to prove how distracted he was, and it had to stop.

He made his way to the tiny space beneath the stairs that he'd commandeered for his office and unlocked the door. The papers were on his desk and he handed them to Matthias. 'That's the full list. Each packing case is labelled so it should be easy enough to check everything off.'

'I just need one copy.' Matthias peeled apart the sheets and handed back the rest. 'I shall despatch a driver immediately to collect the consignment. Do you want it brought here or taken to the hostel.'

'Here… No, the hostel… I'm not sure.' Adam took a deep breath to clear the fug from his head. He had to get a grip if he was to avoid making a fool of himself again. 'Bring everything here. And tell the driver to come and find me when he arrives. I'll get one of the team to sort out the best place to store everything until we can get set up.'

'Fine.' Matthias folded the paper and tucked it into his pocket but his expression was grave when he looked up. 'I may be speaking out of turn but you need to resolve this problem you have with Dr Harris. You are both under enough stress without making your lives even more difficult.'

Adam sighed after Matthias left. He knew that in other circumstances he would have advocated the same course of action. Talking about a problem was usually the best way to resolve it, but he really couldn't see it helping in this instance. The last thing he wanted was to rake up his past mistakes so he would just have to start thinking and acting like the team leader again—put aside his personal feelings and make sure he got the best out of everyone.

He'd had enough practice over the years, so it shouldn't be *that* difficult.

Kasey was in the treatment room when he went back to check on Amelia. She was talking to the little girl so he waited by the door, not wanting to interrupt her. Not surprisingly, the child had been very traumatised when she'd been brought in. She'd lost a lot of blood and had been in a great deal of pain, too, but the fluids and pain relief had kicked in now. He saw Amelia smile shyly when Kasey bent to tenderly stroke her hair and felt a rush of longing suddenly hit him. He would give ten years of his life if only he could have her touch *him* that way!

Kasey suddenly looked up and saw him standing by the door, and his heart ached when he saw the warmth immediately disappear from her eyes to be replaced by wariness. She was on her guard now she knew he was there and he found it unbearably painful to know that. He didn't want to fight with her. He wanted to feel the way he'd done five years ago, happy and exhilarated, filled with his love for her…

His breath caught when it struck him what he was doing. He really couldn't believe that he'd thought such a thing! There was no going back and no way he would want to do so either. Kasey had played him for a fool once already and he wasn't going to give her a second chance to destroy his life. Maybe he was still attracted to her but that was all it was—physical attraction, the most basic of all human emotions, and he would get over it. Eventually. He had to, because there was no place in his life or his heart for a woman like Kasey Harris.

Kasey felt a shiver skip down her spine when she saw the way Adam was looking at her. Since the night they'd operated on the man with the gunshot wounds, she'd deliberately kept out of his way. Maybe it was silly to be so chary, but hearing him state that he wouldn't put her life at risk had made her feel incredibly defenseless, so she'd made up her mind to spend as little time as possible around him.

Fortunately, she'd found herself rostered to work with David Preston most of the time. David had been a little terse with her at first and she'd guessed that he'd taken note of Adam's remarks and had been worried in case she couldn't do her job properly. However, after a couple of stints in Theatre together he'd started to relax, and last night he'd seemed more than happy when she'd volunteered to help him with that emergency case. Slowly but surely she was being accepted by the team and if it weren't for Adam's continued hostility, everything would be fine. However, he seemed determined to think the worst of her.

'How's she doing?' he asked, coming over to the bed.

'Fine. BP is levelling off and her sats are greatly improved.' She rattled off the figures—pulse, BP, oxygen saturation levels—because it was easier to focus on their patient than his inability to accept her as part of the team.

'The fluids and pain relief have obviously helped, so are you happy for me to go ahead and operate,' he asked with punctilious politeness.

'Yes, sir.' Kasey smiled at the girl, ignoring the way his brows drew together when she addressed him as 'sir'. If he wanted professionalism, that's what he'd get from now on. In spades! 'That's what you want, too, isn't it, Amelia?'

'Yes.' The girl smiled shyly at them. 'I want my feet made better.'

Adam's expression was set as he bent and looked at the girl. 'I shall do everything I can, Amelia, but you have to be really brave. I won't be able to make your right foot better again and your left foot is very badly hurt, I'm afraid.'

Kasey saw tears well into Amelia's eyes. Reaching over the bed, she plucked a tissue from the dispenser and wiped her eyes, wondering why he'd told her that. To her mind, it had been little short of cruel to have dashed the child's hopes that way. Something of what she was thinking must have shown on her face because Adam drew her aside.

'I know what you're thinking but it's best not to make promises you can't possibly keep,' he said flatly. 'She has to understand that I can't make her whole again, otherwise she'll never come to terms with what has happened to her.'

'But she's only a child!' Kasey protested. 'Couldn't you at least have tried to explain it to her a bit more gently?'

'No. Her right foot is gone. That's a fact. Her left one is so badly damaged that I won't even rate my chances of putting it back together, let alone lay odds on her being able to walk on it in the future.'

His eyes held hers fast and she saw the pain they held and realised with a start that he was nowhere near as detached as he was pretending to be. 'I wish I could perform miracles, Kasey, but I can't. I can only do my best and in a case like this it falls far short of what any of us would like to do for the poor child.'

'You're right. And I'm sorry.' She sighed when his brows rose. 'You'd think I'd have got over this desire to cure everyone by now, wouldn't you?'

'Don't apologise because you want what is best for your patients,' he said gruffly. 'If you don't aim high then you'll never achieve anything worthwhile.'

'But there's no point aiming for the impossible, is there? Amelia's right foot is gone and the other is in a mess. You were right to make sure she understood that.'

'Maybe. Maybe not.' He shrugged. 'Just because I think it's the best approach, it doesn't mean it's right in this instance. As you pointed out, she's only a child so maybe I should have tried to soften the blow.'

She stared at him in amazement. 'You're not saying that you think you might have been wrong?'

'It has been known.' A wash of colour ran up his face. 'I was wrong to berate you earlier for taking a break and I apologise for it. Daniel told me that you'd been working last night and yet you still turned up on time this morning to do your shift.'

'Of course I did,' she said crisply, trying not to let him see how stunned she was by his apology. It had sounded sincere enough, so what had made him take her to task in the first place if all it had needed were a few words from Daniel to straighten things out?

'There's no ''of course'' about it. However, I don't want you running yourself into the ground by doing more than your share. We have rotas for a reason so it would make more sense if you stuck to them in the future.'

Kasey immediately felt herself bridling. What was the point of him apologising if in the next breath he was telling her off? 'I offered to assist David last night because I thought it would help to cement our working relationship. It was hard enough to gain his trust after what you said the other night so don't you dare start telling me off.'

'What I said?' he repeated darkly. 'Would you care to elaborate?'

'You made it perfectly clear that you didn't want me working with you when you operated on the man with the gunshot injury. Obviously, that put doubts in people's minds about my ability, hence David's initial wariness about working with me.'

'I see. Then it looks like I owe you another apology, doesn't it? Please, take it as read.'

He strode back to the bed, picking up Amelia's chart and making a note on it. Kasey bit her lip. She hated being made to feel as though she'd been whining. She hadn't told him that to drum up sympathy, certainly didn't want him to think it had been a poor-little-me story, but that's how he'd made her feel. She went back to the bed, determined that no matter what he said from now on, she wouldn't react. Cool, calm and completely professional would be her maxim in the future, and if he didn't like it, that was tough!

'You can start the pre-med whenever you're ready.' Adam hung the clipboard on the end of the metal bedstead then glanced at her. 'I'll tell David that I need Theatre and take her straight there. It will disrupt the list but we can't afford to wait any longer.'

'Fine. When will our own equipment arrive, do you know?' she asked, picking up the chart and noting down the pre-medication drugs she would use so they could keep an accurate record of the child's treatment.

'It's already here. Matthias has sent a truck to the airfield to collect it. Once we have the theatre tent set up, we'll be able to run two surgical teams—one in the hospital and the other under canvas. That should speed things up considerably.'

'Good.' She hung the notes back on the bed. 'I'll just have a word with Amelia's parents and tell them what's happening, then get her ready for you.'

'Thank you.' He half turned to leave then paused and she looked expectantly at him.

'Yes?'

'Nothing. I'll see you in Theatre.'

He didn't say anything else as he strode away. Kasey frowned as she watched the door close behind him. She'd had the distinct impression that he'd wanted to say something but had stopped at the last moment.

She sighed as it struck her that it had probably been another reprimand, only he'd thought better of it this time. As far as Adam was concerned she was more a liability than a help, so all she could do was ignore him and get on with her job. After all, she'd worked with other surgeons who'd been equally demanding and survived, although none of them had shared the kind of history she and Adam shared.

That's what it all came down to, of course, not her ability or even the lack of it. It was what she'd done five years ago that had caused this rift and it would continue to cause problems until she managed to resolve the issue. The big question was, what could she do? Just how did you make amends for breaking someone's heart?

CHAPTER FOUR

'I'LL just tidy this up first. Hopefully, once the wound has healed, we'll be able to see about getting her fitted with a prosthetic foot.'

Adam bent over the operating table and carefully removed some sharp splinters of bone which had broken off the end of the tibia. They were three hours into the operation to repair Amelia's injuries and there was at least another hour's work before he could finish off, but everyone seemed to be holding up.

He dropped the splinters into a dish, nodding his thanks when Lorraine moved it out of his way. It had made a huge difference having such a skilled team to work with and he appreciated the efforts everyone had made to remain focused despite the gruelling conditions they were working under. There was no air-conditioning in the hospital's theatre and the heat was appalling, but there'd been no complaints. Everyone had just buckled down and got the job done, from the nursing staff to Kasey, who was acting as his anaesthetist. She'd been particularly alert to any possible problems and had maintained a constant vigil over the child. It made him feel incredibly guilty to know that he'd cast doubts in people's minds about her ability. Kasey had always been a superb anaesthetist and he had to credit her for that if nothing else.

He glanced towards the head of the operating table, where Kasey was seated beside the old-fashioned machinery. 'How's she doing?'

'BP stable, heart rate and breathing both steady,' she replied politely.

'Excellent!' he replied heartily. 'You've done a really great job maintaining her.'

'Thank you.'

He sighed when he heard the cool note in her voice. It sounded as though his compliment had been too little, too late. He couldn't blame her if she was annoyed with him for putting doubts in people's minds—it would have irked him, too, if the situation had been reversed. He realised that he had to do something to address the problem and decided to have a word with everyone over dinner that night. A slice of humble pie should round off the meal!

He carried on with what he was doing, removing sections of bone from the lower part of Amelia's right leg but leaving enough skin and muscle to provide a pad to cover the stump. Blood vessels had to be tied off and nerves severed well above the site of the amputation to reduce pressure pain in the future. Mercifully, Amelia's left foot hadn't been as badly damaged as he'd feared: although she'd lost three of her toes, she should be able to walk on it eventually. All in all, the child had been extremely lucky—at least she hadn't been killed by the explosion and she should still be able to get around—so he felt far more upbeat after he'd put the final suture in place.

'That's it, then. With a bit of luck, she'll be up and about in a few weeks time.' He smiled around the table. 'A first-rate job performed under very trying circumstances. Thank you, everyone.'

'Our pleasure,' June replied cheerfully, busily checking off the instruments they'd used. She handed the last few items to Lorraine then helped her push the rickety old trolley out of Theatre. Fortunately, the hospital's autoclave was still functioning so they'd been able to use it to sterilise their instruments.

Adam stretched his aching back as he stepped away from the table. Kasey was reversing the anaesthetic now and he glanced at her. 'If everything's all right here, I'll go and take a shower. Mary promised to get a bed ready in that side room off the main ward so I'll ask her to come and fetch Amelia.'

'There's no need. I want to be sure that she's come round fully from the anaesthetic before I hand her over so I'll take her through myself when she's ready.'

'You need a break, Kasey. Mary is perfectly capable of keeping an eye on her from now on.'

'I'm sure she is. However, Amelia is my patient and I have no intention of handing over responsibility for her until I'm sure she's recovered sufficiently.'

She stared back at him, her beautiful face betraying so little emotion that for some reason Adam felt his own emotions bubbling up to the surface. It took every scrap of willpower he possessed not to let them spill over.

'If that's your decision, who am I to disagree?' he said in a voice that sounded far harsher than he'd intended it to.

He left Theatre and headed for the showers, stripping off his sweat-soaked scrub suit and unceremoniously stuffing it into the dirty linen hamper. Grabbing a towel off the shelf, he stepped into a cubicle, cursing roundly when he turned on the taps and a dribble of cold water leaked from the shower head. He twisted the dial this way and that but he still couldn't persuade the shower to work any better.

Leaving the first cubicle, he tried the next one and achieved the same result: a couple of drops of cold water and that was all. It looked as though something had gone wrong with their water supply and it was the final straw on top of everything else that had happened that day. Why in the name of all that was holy had he ever agreed to run this mission in the first place?

Dragging on his clothes, he left the changing room. Tony Bridges, their physician, was coming along the cor-

ridor and said something to him in passing but Adam
didn't pause. He strode out of the main doors and climbed
into the Jeep, gunning the engine and sending a flock of
birds scattering from the nearby trees. It was a ten minute
drive from the hospital to the hostel and he did it in six,
drawing up outside with a squeal of tyres. He couldn't
remember ever feeling so angry and frustrated before...
apart from that night when Kasey had told him the truth,
of course.

His mouth compressed as he entered the building. Every
single thing that happened lately seemed to revolve around
Kasey. He'd thought he'd got over her, honestly believed
that he'd put it all behind him, but he'd been wrong. The
memory had been festering inside him all these years, and
the thought of what could happen if it erupted scared him
rigid. There was no way that he was going to put himself
through that kind of torment again!

He took the stairs two at a time and flung open his
bedroom door. He needed to think about what had gone
on five years ago because that had been his biggest mistake, of course: he'd tried to block out the pain by burying
himself in work instead of dealing with it. But if he was
to survive, he had to start right back at the beginning,
exorcise those ghosts from the past so he could start living
again in the present.

Lying down on the bed, he closed his eyes and opened
his mind, unsurprised when Kasey immediately flowed
in...

'Hi! I'm Kasey Harris, your new anaesthetist.'

*Adam swung round when he heard a lilting voice behind
him. He'd just left Theatre after a particularly gruelling
session and the last thing he felt like doing was making
conversation with the newcomer. The cool dismissal was*

already forming on his lips when his eyes alighted on the woman standing in front of him and he froze.

Silky black curls swirled around a delicate oval face; deep blue eyes gleamed with warmth and another emotion too subtle to put a name to but one which made his senses respond on some subliminal level. When she held out a slender hand, he found himself reaching for it like a drowning man.

'And you must be Adam Chandler, of course!'

Her hand gripped his, her soft palm pressed to his hard one, the pads of her fingers exerting the most delicate pressure on the back of his hand, and he almost groaned out loud in ecstasy. It was just a handshake, yet it felt as though every nerve in his body was suddenly transfixed with pleasure. It was only when he saw the faintly quizzical lift of her brows that he realised he should really let her go.

'Sorry. I'm a bit spaced out at the moment, I'm afraid.' His hand fell to his side and he felt the loss of contact like a physical ache in his gut. It shocked him so much that he rushed on. 'Twelve hours in Theatre tends to do that to you.'

'I know. I've had some spaced out moments of my own,' she replied sympathetically. 'Although the rush you get afterwards from a job well done makes up for it, doesn't it?'

'It certainly does.'

It was so exactly how he'd always felt that he had to stop himself grinning inanely at her. He glanced at his watch, feigning an impatience to be off because the alternative—standing there for the rest of his days while he savoured her beauty—simply wasn't possible.

'I can see that you're busy so I won't detain you,' she said lightly, taking the hint. 'Far be it from me to get between a surgeon and his scalpel!'

Adam summoned a smile when he heard the teasing note in her voice, although he couldn't remember the last time anyone had spoken to him that way, and certainly not a member of staff. They were far too in awe of him to behave so familiarly but Kasey Harris obviously didn't view him in the same light as everyone else.

How exactly did she see him? he wondered curiously, then hastily stifled the thought. He really didn't want to go down that road.

'Anyway, I just thought I'd introduce myself. I'm not actually due to start work until tomorrow so I expect I'll see you then...' She left the sentence open and he immediately jumped into the gap.

'I'm not rostered tomorrow, I'm afraid. I have a few days' leave owing to me so I'll be off for the rest of the week, in fact.'

'Oh, I see. What a shame.' She sounded as though she genuinely regretted his absence and he couldn't deny that it was a wonderful boost to his ego.

'It is.' He smiled even more warmly at her this time. 'Maybe we could make up for it by going out for dinner one night while I'm off?'

'Why, I'd love to! I've only just moved to London so I'm at a bit of a loose end with having to leave all my friends behind in Dublin.'

'Oh, so you're Irish? I thought I detected a certain lilt in your voice.'

'I was born in Ireland, although I moved to England many years ago after my mother remarried so that's probably how I lost most of my accent. I went back there to study, though, and ended up staying on after I qualified.' She grimaced. 'I really mustn't keep you here chatting. You must have loads of things to do. When would you like us to meet for that dinner?'

'Would tomorrow night be OK for you?'

He named a restaurant and they fixed a time before she hurried away. Adam sighed as he watched her walking along the corridor. Now that the initial feeling of euphoria was starting to fade, he couldn't help wondering if he'd been mad to ask her out like that. He'd made it a strict rule never to get involved with the people he worked with. It had meant that his social life had been a bit restricted because he spent more time at work than anywhere else, but at least he'd avoided any unpleasantness when a relationship had broken up. Yet within two minutes of meeting Kasey Harris he'd invited her out to dinner and he wasn't sure if it had been the most sensible thing to do.

He took a half-step to go after her when she suddenly turned, and even from that distance he could see the smile in her eyes. When she raised her hand and waved to him, he waved back. Adam took a deep breath as she disappeared from sight but his heart was racing and other parts of his anatomy were performing manoeuvres normally confined to the privacy of his bedroom! He knew then that there wasn't a chance of him cancelling their date. He was going to meet Kasey Harris the following night and simply see what happened...

'Adam! Adam, wake up!'

His eyelids flickered open when he heard Kasey calling his name. The dream had been so vivid that he wasn't the least surprised when he found her bending over him. Catching hold of her hand, he pulled her down towards him.

'Good morning,' he murmured as his lips found hers. He kissed her slowly, lingeringly, while his free hand moved to her breast, sighing with pleasure when her nipple immediately peaked...

'For heaven's sake, stop that!'

She pushed him away and Adam's eyes opened properly

this time, opened and absorbed what he was actually seeing, which was Kasey glaring at him, her face flushed, her
beautiful mouth quivering not with passion, as he'd expected but with what looked very much like anger to him.
Pushing himself upright on the bed, he did a quick reality
check and only just managed not to groan out loud when
he realised what he'd done. He'd allowed that dream to
spill over into waking time and it was galling to imagine
what Kasey must be thinking.

'Sorry,' he said brusquely, standing up. 'I thought you
were someone else.'

'Obviously!' she snapped, but he saw the flicker of pain
that crossed her face before she turned away.

Adam was sorely tempted to ask her what was wrong,
but he knew he couldn't afford to ask a question like that
in case she reciprocated. The thought of having to come
up with an identity for the mystery woman he'd claimed
to have been dreaming about was more than he could cope
with.

'So what's all the panic about?' he demanded instead,
hating the fact that he'd felt it necessary to lie. There was
no woman in his life and hadn't been for a very long time
now. It was ages since he'd been out on a date never mind
anything else and the thought did little to soothe him.

What would Kasey think if she found out that he hadn't
slept with another woman since they'd split up? he wondered bitterly. Would she be amused at the thought of his
continued celibacy or merely pity him for not getting over
what had happened? Neither option was one that he particularly relished, and he glared at her.

'Well? Spit it out. I assume you have a good reason for
barging into my room.'

'Matthias has been shot.' She took a gulping breath and
he could tell that she was struggling to regain her com-
posure. 'Apparently, he decided to go to the airfield to help

the driver load our equipment onto the truck and they were ambushed on their way back. The driver managed to get away and brought him straight to the hospital so that's why I came to fetch you.'

'Hell!' Adam was out of the door in a trice, his booted feet thundering on the floorboards as he raced along the landing. 'How badly hurt is he?' he demanded over his shoulder.

'It's a gut wound,' she told him flatly, and he winced. 'David was still trying to stabilise him when I left. He'll take him straight to Theatre once that's done, but it didn't look too good from what I saw.'

'Gunshot wounds to the gut are the worst of all,' he said grimly, racing down the stairs. 'There's so much scope for soft tissue damage that they're always the hardest to deal with.'

He stopped when they reached the hall, seeing the shock that was etched on her face and hating the fact that he was powerless to do anything about it. He made himself focus on practicalities instead, because if he didn't then he was afraid that he would do something really stupid, like taking her in his arms.

'We need to find Sarah and tell her what's happened.'

'Sarah?'

'Matthias's wife. They live on the other side of town but I'm not sure exactly where because I've not been to their house yet. Damn and blast!' he exclaimed as his frustration spilled over. 'Why didn't I ask Matthias for directions?'

'You weren't to know this would happen. This whole area is supposed to be fairly safe now that the fighting has stopped.'

'So safe that someone got shot the first night we arrived,' he pointed out sharply because he didn't want Kasey helping him out when he couldn't return the favour.

He led the way outside and climbed into the Jeep, glancing round when she jumped in beside him. 'There's no need for you to go back to the hospital. Your shift must be over by now so you may as well stay here.'

'I want to go back. Even if there isn't much I can do for Matthias, at least I can try and find out where he lives. Maybe one of the patients knows or the truck driver. He was still there when I left and he might have waited so I'll ask him.'

'I suppose so,' he conceded grudgingly, letting in the clutch. 'I know that Matthias has been treating people from his own home during the fighting so someone must know where he lives.'

'Exactly. And once I find out, I can go and fetch Sarah—'

'No. I absolutely forbid it, Kasey. It's far too dangerous for you to drive around the town on your own.'

'I'm going whether you agree or not.' She half turned in the seat so she could look at him, putting up her hand to hold back her hair as the wind whipped it across her face.

'Then you can pack your bags as soon as you get back.'

He gripped the steering-wheel with both hands, aware that he was handling the situation badly. Normally, he wouldn't have dreamt of taking such a stance but would have dealt with the issue calmly and with reason, pointing out why it was such a bad idea. However, calm and reason were two commodities in short supply when it came to dealing with Kasey.

'I am in charge of this team and my word is law. If you expressly flout my orders then I shall have no choice but to send you back to England.'

'And that would solve your problem perfectly, wouldn't it?' She plucked a strand of hair out of her mouth and laughed. 'Nobody could blame you for sending me back under those circumstances, could they, Adam? I'd be classified as a loose cannon, a liability, and the agency would remove me from their files and that would be it. All nice and tidy, just how you like it.'

'Yes! You're right. It would give me the greatest satisfaction to send you home because you've done nothing but cause me problems ever since you joined this team.' He drew up in front of the hospital and set the handbrake before he turned to her.

'I never wanted you to come in the first place and you know why, too. The only thing I don't understand is why you decided to come along when you found out I was leading this team. Did it give you a perverse kind of pleasure to disrupt my life again? Or were you still trying to pay me back for what I supposedly did to your brother? Come on, Kasey, don't hold back. You certainly weren't shy about telling me the truth five years ago.'

'I thought it would help.'

'Help?' He laughed harshly. 'Help who? Please, don't tell me you were doing this for me.'

'I thought it would help *me* get over what happened!'

The wind whipped her hair out of her hand so that he couldn't see her face. He had to rely on what he was hearing and the pain in her voice lanced straight through his heart.

'You weren't the only one who got hurt, Adam. It was just as bad for me as it was for you.'

'Just as bad for you... What the hell do you mean by that?'

He could barely speak for the knot in his throat so that his voice sounded like steel drums being bounced over rocks. He saw her bite her lip as she flicked back her hair and had to clench his hands to stop himself touching her. He mustn't do that and certainly mustn't make the mistake of feeling sorry for her. He had to remember how she'd tricked him once before, yet it was hard to hold onto that thought when he saw how devastated she looked.

'Telling you the truth that night was the hardest thing I've ever had to do, and not a day has passed since then when I've not thought about it. I know I hurt you, Adam, and I know that in the beginning it was what I wanted to do, but I never realised that it would be so painful for me, too.'

She brushed her hand over her eyes and his heart ached even more when he saw the tears that were trembling on her lashes. It was all he could do to make himself sit there and not say a word.

'You see, I had feelings for you, too, Adam. It wasn't all an act as you seem to believe.'

Blood roared through his head when he suddenly realised what she'd said, so that for a moment his vision blurred. Did she really think he was stupid enough to fall for that?

It seemed too incredible to be true, yet when his vision eventually cleared, he could tell that was exactly what she was hoping for and for some reason he didn't know what to do. He knew that he should have laughed in her face and told her that there wasn't a chance in hell of him falling for her lies a second time, yet he couldn't quite bring himself to do that...

He flung open the Jeep door, terrified that he would make another terrible mistake if he remained there even a second longer. Lorraine must have been watching for them to arrive because she met him at the top of the steps and hurried him straight to the treatment room.

Adam grabbed the gloves June held out to him and went straight to the bed, rapping out orders to right and left, focusing every bit of his mind on the only thing that mattered at that moment, which was saving Matthias's life. He didn't intend to waste time thinking about Kasey and the pain she'd caused him in the past and would cause him again if he let her. He certainly didn't intend to let himself wonder if maybe—possibly—*perhaps*—she'd been telling him the truth just now. He might be many things but he wasn't that much of a fool, so help him!

'Can someone do a cut-down? We need to get some more fluids into him, stat! He's lost so much blood that I can't find a decent vein in his arm.'

Kasey turned away, unable to bear to watch any more as the team continued their fight to save Matthias. David and Adam were still trying to stabilise him before they could take him through to Theatre. Joan Simpson, their expert on dengue fever, was currently cross matching blood for a desperately needed transfusion while Gordon Thompson had abandoned his typhus clinic and was now doing the cut-down—delicately slicing through the skin in Matthias's ankle to find a viable vein. Daniel was in Theatre, getting everything ready, while the rest of the team were keeping things ticking over. She was the only one who didn't have a proper role in the proceedings. Unless she opted for the one she'd chosen for herself.

Her heart thumped as she went back into the corridor. She knew that Adam would carry out his threat to send her home if she went to find Sarah, but maybe it wouldn't be such a bad thing after all. Blurting out that she'd had feelings for him five years ago had been a really stupid thing to do and she hadn't needed his lack of response to tell her that. All she could do now was thank her lucky stars that he hadn't questioned her because she had no idea what she would have told him: that she'd fallen in love with him and had her heart broken as well?

Oh, please!

She strode along the corridor, furious with herself for making such a mess of everything. If she was sent home then so be it, but she was going to accomplish something before she went. Fortunately, the truck driver was still in the hospital, waiting for news of Matthias, so she went to find him. He was sitting at the nursing station, drinking a cup of tea, and he leapt to his feet as soon as she appeared.

'How is Dr Matthias, missie?'

'He's still in the treatment room,' Kasey explained. 'Dr Adam is going to operate as soon as they manage to stabilise him.'

'I did everything I could,' the man said anxiously. 'As soon as they started firing at us, I drove as fast as I could.'

'I'm sure it wasn't your fault,' she said soothingly.

She glanced round when June came bustling back for some more dressings and led him away from the desk so they wouldn't be overheard. Even though Adam was busy with his patient, he would find a way to stop her if he discovered that she was about to flout his orders. Her heart hiccuped at the thought of how he was going to react when he found out, but she couldn't afford to let it deter her.

She smiled at the driver. 'It's Lester, isn't it?'

'That's right, missie.' Lester took a shiny new identity card out of his pocket and proudly pointed to his photograph. 'Dr Matthias appointed me as his head driver and told me that I must always carry this badge with me to prove who I am.'

'That's excellent, Lester.' Kasey admired the badge then handed it back to him. 'I don't suppose you know where Dr Matthias lives, do you?'

'Of course. He lives on the other side of town, near to where I lived when I was a little child.' He smiled broadly when she gasped, obviously delighted by her reaction.

'Oh, that's wonderful! Then you can you tell me how to get there, can't you?'

'No, no. It is not safe for you to go there, missie,' Lester said anxiously. 'There are too many bad people about.'

'What if you came with me?' she suggested quickly. 'It would be safer if there were two of us and much easier if I had you along to show me the way. I don't know my way round the town like you do so I could get lost.'

'I don't know… Maybe Dr Adam wouldn't be happy about you going there. I wouldn't like to do anything to upset him so perhaps you should ask him first.'

Kasey shook her head. She already knew what Adam's answer would be. 'Dr Adam is very busy at the moment and I don't want to bother him. I shall take full responsibility, Lester, so you don't have to worry about getting into trouble. We'll take the Jeep instead of the truck because it will be quicker.'

She bustled Lester towards the door before he could raise any more objections. There was nobody about when they left the hospital and she breathed a sigh of relief. Adam had left the keys in the ignition—an unprecedented move for someone who was normally so careful, but then he had been rather upset at the time.

Kasey started the engine, refusing to think about why Adam had been so upset. They left the hospital and she followed Lester's directions as they drove through the town. They came to a junction and she automatically slowed down in case there was any other traffic coming, but Lester shook his head.

'No, no, miss. Keep driving. Don't stop. It's too dangerous.'

Kasey's stomach churned when he pointed to a gang of youths loitering near the remains of a burnt out truck. They were eyeing the Jeep with interest so she stamped on the accelerator and they shot across the junction. Lester told her to make a left turn and her nervousness increased as they drove along a series of increasingly narrow side streets, lined on both sides with tumbled-down buildings. There were a lot of people about and they all stopped to watch as she drove past. By the time they reached Matthias's house she was starting to wish she'd never set out on the journey and the thought of having to drive all the way back wasn't something she relished.

She switched off the engine and turned to Lester. 'I'll see if Sarah is home.'

'And I shall stay here and look after the Jeep,' Lester told her, looking around nervously.

'I'll be as quick as I can,' she assured him, scrambling out of the Jeep.

She hurried up the path and banged on the front door of the tiny, tin-roofed bungalow. In contrast to some of the areas they'd driven through, this part of the town seemed relatively quiet. There were just a few people about and no sign of the gangs that had alarmed her so much. She knocked on the door again then jumped when it suddenly opened and a tall, slender black woman appeared.

'Sarah?'

'Yes.' The woman's face broke into a sudden smile. 'You must be one of the doctors from the hospital! I'm so glad that Matthias has brought you to our house at last. I've been begging him to invite you all round for dinner—'

'Sarah, Matthias hasn't brought me here. I came on my own.' Kasey reached out and gripped Sarah's hands, seeing the fear that suddenly clouded her eyes.

'Something has happened. It's Matthias, isn't it? He's—'

'He's been shot. He's in the hospital and he's going to need an operation,' Kasey said quickly, squeezing her hands. 'He's very poorly but he was alive when I left.'

'He's alive!' Sarah suddenly slumped against the wall and would have fallen if Kasey hadn't grabbed her.

'Yes, and I'm going to take you to see him. Do you think you can walk to the car?'

'Yes… Of course. I'm sorry… It was just the shock…'

Sarah made a courageous effort to pull herself together and Kasey smiled at her. 'You're doing great. Let's just get you into the car.'

She took Sarah's arm and helped her to the Jeep. Once Sarah was settled, she got in and started the engine. It was already starting to go dark and she knew that night would fall before they reached the hospital.

She turned the vehicle around and headed back the way they'd come, glad of Lester's help because everywhere looked so different in the dark. They came to the junction again and she didn't need his encouragement this time as she floored the accelerator. One glance at the gang of young men standing on the corner was enough to tell her that it would be a mistake to linger. It was a relief when they reached the hospital and she pulled up in front of the main doors. Switching off the engine, she turned to Lester with a smile of thanks, which faded abruptly when a figure suddenly appeared from inside the building.

Kasey's heart felt like a yo-yo being jerked about on its string as she watched Adam walking towards them, because even in the darkness she could tell that he was furious. He didn't even glance at her as he opened the door and helped Sarah out.

'Matthias has just left Theatre,' he told Sarah without any preamble. 'He's very ill but he's alive.'

'Oh, thank you, thank you.' Tears flowed down Sarah's cheeks and Adam put his arm around her shoulders.

'I'll take you straight in to see him,' he said gently, so gently, in fact, that Kasey felt her own eyes fill with tears because she knew he wasn't going to treat her so tenderly.

She followed them inside, thanking Lester for his help and assuring him that he wasn't in any trouble. Once she'd dealt with him, she went to find Adam because there was no point putting it off. He was waiting outside his office for her and he didn't say a word as he ushered her inside.

Kasey sat down in front of the desk because it seemed wiser to be seated when the full weight of his wrath descended on her. Adam closed the door then sat down and the very quietness of his actions warned her just how angry he was. Picking up a manila folder, he took out a sheet of paper and pushed it across the desk towards her.

'This terminates your contract with the agency. All you need to do is sign it at the bottom. I'm not sure when we shall be able to fly you home. It depends when the next delivery of supplies is scheduled to arrive. In the meantime, you are relieved of your duties—'

'No way!' Kasey pushed the form away. 'I'm willing to accept that you can send me home for disobeying your orders, Adam, but there is no way that I'm going to sit around all day and do nothing until you get rid of me.'

'It isn't up to you to decide what you will and won't do,' he said harshly. His green eyes bored into her and she shivered when she saw the fury they held. 'This is my decision, Dr Harris, and it isn't open for discussion.'

He pushed back his chair, making it clear that the meeting was over, but there was no way that she was going to agree without putting up a fight.

She leapt to her feet. 'And if your decision had been based purely on what I did tonight then I'd accept it, but it wasn't. You've already admitted that you couldn't wait to get rid of me, so at least have the guts not to lie about why you're stopping me from working. It's pettiness, Adam, sheer, bloody-minded pettiness that's behind it!'

He was round the desk in a flash, moving so fast that she barely had time to blink before he was in front of her. Kasey took a step back because the expression on his face was enough to make even the bravest person back down, but he simply hauled her back.

'Have you any idea what could have happened to you?' he bit out savagely.

'I can't imagine it would be much worse than having to put up with the way you've been treating me!' she retorted, hating to feel at such a disadvantage.

He ignored that as he bent and stared into her eyes. 'You could have been shot. You could have been raped. You could even have been kidnapped and held to ransom because that's what happens in countries where the whole infrastructure has broken down. That's three options so how do you fancy any of those?'

He laughed softly when she didn't reply. 'Of course, I'm assuming that anyone would think it was worth bothering with you. They might just have killed you and taken the Jeep because it's worth far more than some foolish woman who doesn't have the sense to understand what she's getting herself into.'

'That's enough! I know you're angry, Adam—'

'No, you don't. You have no idea how I feel.'

He hauled her towards him so fast that the breath whooshed from her body as they suddenly collided. Kasey raised her hands to push him away, wanting to set some space between them so she could deal with this rationally, yet the moment her hands touched him, they forgot what they were doing.

Heat flashed along her veins, lightning finding its own special conductor from him to her, and she gasped, heard him gasp as well, felt the tension in the air increase until it seemed as though the whole world would implode on itself. And then his head dipped and his mouth found hers and all the emotions gelled into one overwhelming force, anger and frustration turning to passion in a single beat of her heart.

Adam kissed her and she kissed him back, kissed him and clung to him, murmured his name, wrapped her arms around his neck and held on because she didn't care what had prompted the kiss, only cared that it should continue. And it did. It did!

'Adam, Adam.'

She murmured his name in a frenzy of need, her fingers sliding through the crisp, dark hair on the back of his head, feeling the strong bones of his skull, the heat of his skin, and his mouth moved lower, found her breast, suckled her through her shirt and her bra.

Sensations exploded inside her until she didn't think she could stand any more yet there were many more to come: the first tingling chill of excitement when he stripped off her blouse and bra; the velvet roughness of his tongue on her sensitised nipples; the hardness of his erection pressing against the junction of her thighs; her own dampness...

'No!' He dragged himself away and she flinched when she heard the contempt in his voice. 'I am not letting this happen again!'

'Adam—' she began, her voice trembling with shock and need.

'Here.'

He thrust her blouse and bra towards her and she took them automatically, although her hands were shaking so much that she couldn't manage to put them on. He muttered something harsh as he took the blouse from her again and helped her into it, his touch so impersonal now that she almost laughed. Only, if she gave in to her emotions, she wasn't sure if she'd be able to stop.

He fastened the buttons and stepped back as though he found it repugnant to touch her, and that hurt far more than anything else could have done. This man had just kissed her, caressed her, brought her body and his own to life in the most glorious way possible, yet he could no longer bear to touch her!

She stood up straighter, knowing that the only thing she

had left now was her dignity. 'I can't stop you if you insist on sending me home. However, I want to make it clear that I shall continue to work the shifts I'm rostered for until you can arrange for me to be repatriated.'

'If that's what you wish.' He walked around the desk and sat down. 'As for your future with Worlds Together, it will be up to you to decide if you want to carry on working for them on other missions. I won't put anything in my report about you deliberately ignoring my orders, so your future with the agency won't be compromised in any way.'

'In case I mention what happened afterwards?' She laughed bitterly. 'Don't worry, Adam, it isn't something I'm keen to publicise either so it will be our little secret.'

'If you wish to make a formal complaint about my behaviour tonight, that is your right. I certainly won't try to deny that what I did was wrong.'

His head came up and he stared back at her: Adam Chandler at his most arrogant and daunting.

'And I have no intention of making a complaint.' She held his gaze because she didn't want there to be any mistake about this. 'We both know that I could have stopped you any time I chose to do so, Adam. I wasn't the victim of an unsolicited sexual attack and I have no intention of claiming that I was to get back at you. I take full responsibility for my actions. I always have.'

She swung round and opened the door, pausing when he said softly behind her, 'I'm sorry, though, Kasey. Really sorry.'

'Me, too,' she whispered, although she wasn't sure if he'd heard her, let alone understood what she was apologising for.

She left the office and made her way outside. The Jeep was still parked where she'd left it and she got in. It was just gone eight when she arrived at the hostel and she went straight to her room, relieved that she didn't meet anyone on the way. June was working that night with Mary and everyone else would be in the dining room.

Frankly, the thought of food was more than she could face so she collected her wash-bag and took a shower then got ready for bed. There would be time enough in the morning to tell everyone that she was leaving and, in the meantime, she'd work out some sort of story to explain why she was going. She couldn't possibly tell them the truth, which was that Adam hated her.

Tears welled to her eyes but she blinked them away. She wouldn't say or do anything to show that she was upset. She would behave with dignity throughout the rest of her time in Mwuranda so that nobody would blame Adam when she left. It wasn't his fault that they couldn't work together. It was hers. The wound she'd inflicted on him had gone too deep for him to forgive her and that was what she'd tried to apologise for in the office.

She was truly sorry that she'd hurt him, even though she'd thought it had been justified at the time. Now she could see how wrong it had been to cause him so much pain. Maybe he had hurt her brother, but she was no longer sure if he'd realised how harmful those comments he'd made to Keiran had been.

Adam wasn't deliberately cruel and the proof of that was the fact that he'd stopped tonight when he could so easily have carried on and made love to her. It would have been the perfect way to even the score between them but he hadn't done it.

That hadn't been the action of a cruel man, a bully, and all of a sudden it felt as though she no longer knew what was right or wrong any more. For all this time she'd believed that Adam had shown a blatant and relentless disregard for her brother's feelings, but had he?

It was a question she couldn't answer, and that was the

most difficult thing of all—to suddenly have these doubts when she'd been so certain before. What made it all the more poignant was knowing in her heart that she and Adam could have found real happiness together if only they'd had the chance.

CHAPTER FIVE

'YOUR foot is healing beautifully. You've been a very brave girl, Amelia. We'll soon have you running about again.'

Adam tried to shrug off the despondency that had been his constant companion for the past couple of days as he smiled at the girl. He was in the middle of a ward round so he said goodbye to Amelia and moved to the next bed, sighing when he saw the frosty look June gave him as she handed him the next patient's notes. Although nobody had said anything to him about Kasey's impending departure, it was obvious they blamed him for sending her home because there was a definite chill in the air whenever he was around and it simply added to his overall feeling of self-disgust. He should never have kissed Kasey like that!

His hands shook as he hung the clipboard on the end of the bed and he saw June glance at him. 'Too much coffee, I'm afraid. I'm probably on a caffeine high.'

'Funny, that's what Kasey said as well,' June observed loftily.

Adam folded his arms. 'OK. Spit it out. I can tell you're dying to say something.'

'I just think it's wrong that Kasey should be sent home.' June gave him a gimlet-eyed stare. 'Oh, I know she's told everyone that it was her decision but I don't believe her. And neither does anyone else. She's going home because you're sending her home, isn't she?'

'Yes. Kasey deliberately went against my orders. I warned her what the consequences would be if she went to find Sarah, and she chose to ignore me, so that's why I'm sending her back to England.'

'But nothing happened! She got back safely and she brought Sarah with her. Surely you could reconsider—'

'No.' He shook his head. 'I'm sorry, June, but my decision is final. I cannot have people going off on their own whenever they feel like it. Now, if you don't mind, we need to get on. I do have a full list this morning.'

June didn't say anything else; she remained tight-lipped throughout the rest of the ward round, answering his questions as briefly as possible. Adam didn't make an issue of it even though it was galling to be cast in the role of villain. They came to Matthias's room and he breathed a sigh of relief when June was called away. At least he wouldn't get the cold-shoulder from his friend.

'So how do you feel today?' he asked, glancing at the notes the night staff had made. Despite extensive damage to his large intestine, Matthias was making steady progress. David had performed a colostomy—an operation in which part of the colon is brought through an incision in the abdomen—then removed the section of colon that had been ripped apart when the bullet had entered the body. There'd been a lot of damage to the surrounding tissue and blood vessels so Adam had dealt with that himself, working late into the night to make sure Matthias had had the best chance possible of recovering. It had been worth it because in the last twenty-four hours, they'd updated his status from critical to serious.

'As though I have been gored by a bull.' Matthias smiled weakly when his wife tutted. 'I know, my love. I should not complain when it was my own fault for getting in the way of that bullet.'

'Sounds as though you're in the dog house,' Adam observed with a grin.

'And so he should be,' Sarah said tartly. 'He tells me

not to go out of the house then goes all the way to the airfield with only a driver to help if they encounter trouble!'

'The way to hell is paved with my good intentions.' Matthias smiled at his wife. 'But you still love me so that is all that matters.'

'I give up!' Sarah stood up. 'I shall go and see if one of the nurses can spare a few minutes to talk to me. At least I will enjoy some sensible conversation then!'

She swept out of the room and Matthias sighed. 'She must have been so frightened when she found out what had happened to me. I shall never forgive myself for that.'

'The best way to make amends is to get better,' Adam told him rousingly. 'And from the look of this chart, you seem to be making excellent progress.'

'Thanks to you and David. I owe you both my life and I shall never forget that. Nor will I forget what Dr Harris did. Going to fetch Sarah was a very brave thing to do.'

Adam shook his head when he heard the reproof in Matthias's voice. 'If you're going to tell me that I've been too hard on her, save your breath. She should never have driven all that way on her own.'

'No, she shouldn't. But I hate to think that I have been the cause of this...disharmony.'

Adam laughed. 'You aren't to blame. Kasey and I have a history of disharmony, as you so delicately put it.'

'Is that why you are sending her home? Not because of what she did the other day but because of something that happened in the past?'

'It probably didn't help,' he admitted truthfully. 'But sending her back to England is for her own good. Anything could have happened to her the other night. You know that as well as I do.'

'Ah! So it's because you care about her?' Matthias said rather smugly.

'Don't go putting words into my mouth. I'm sending Dr Harris home because she can't follow orders. Period!'

'Excuse me.'

Adam's heart sank when he turned and found Kasey standing behind him. It was obvious that she'd overheard what he'd said. He'd seen very little of her since the other night. When he'd come into work the following day, he'd discovered that she'd altered the rosters so that she could work with David from then on. He could have objected, of course, because it wasn't up to her to make such changes, but it hadn't seemed worth making a fuss. The less time they spent around each other until she returned to England, the easier it would be, he'd reasoned, so it was galling to have been caught discussing her like that.

'Did you want me?' he asked rather too sharply.

'There's a woman in Reception who wants to speak to you. I told her you were busy but she was adamant that she has to see you.'

'Did she tell you what it was about?'

'No. She refused to tell me anything else.'

'Then you'd better show her to my office.' He checked his watch. 'If you're not needed in Theatre, could you stay with her? I should only be a couple of minutes now.'

'Of course.'

Adam sighed as he watched her walk away. Once again he'd handled the situation badly. There'd been no need to be so abrupt with her when she'd been merely passing on a message. He needed to address this problem before she left, because the last thing he wanted was for them to part on such bad terms.

The thought startled him because it really shouldn't matter what Kasey thought of him. Her opinion should have been the least of his problems yet he was too honest to lie to himself. He did his best not to dwell on it while he examined Matthias, however, because he didn't want anything to spoil his concentration in case he missed something vital. Peritonitis was always a major concern in a case like this. Once bacteria escaped from the intestine and spilled into the abdominal cavity, it could cause inflammation of the peritoneum—the membrane lining the abdominal cavity and covering the abdominal organs. It was something he was anxious to avoid so he carefully felt Matthias's abdomen, checking for any signs of tension or bloating, but everything appeared to be fine. The fact that his friend's temperature was normal and that he'd not been vomiting were also good signs. Stripping off his gloves, he gave Matthias the good news as he washed his hands.

'Everything is looking very positive, I'm pleased to say. We'll close the wound in a couple of days but I think you're going to avoid most of the usual complications.'

'Put it down to clean living,' Matthias joked.

'How about the skill of the surgical team?' Adam countered. 'Not to mention all the nursing care you've received.'

'Hmm, I suppose that did have something to do with it,' Matthias agreed with a smile. 'You have an excellent team working here, Adam. Every single person is so highly skilled. It would be a shame to lose any of them for whatever reason.'

Adam raised an eyebrow. 'This wouldn't be another attempt to get me to change my mind about Kasey, would it?'

'Yes. She's good at her job, she gets on well with the rest of the team and—'

'And she has a problem following orders.' He shook his head. 'Sorry, but my mind is made up and nothing you can say will make me change it. Dr Harris will be flown home as soon as I can get her on a plane.'

He bade Matthias goodbye and left the ward, pausing only long enough to tell June that he was needed in the office and after that he would be in Theatre. Their own theatre tent had been set up in the grounds of the hospital now so they'd been able to double the workload. David had decided to stay in the hospital's theatre, leaving the mobile unit to him. It suited Adam fine because there was less risk of him bumping into Kasey if he spent most of his time outside the building.

It was disquieting to admit that he'd tailored his working life to fit around Kasey because he wasn't used to having to compromise. As he strode into his office, he promised himself that once she'd left, he would get back to normal. Kasey was sitting in his chair and she stood up when he appeared, but he waved her back to her seat as he introduced himself to the blonde-haired woman occupying the other chair.

'I'm Adam Chandler. I believe you wanted to speak to me.'

'Claire Morgan.' She stood up to shake hands with him and he was surprised to see that she was wearing what looked very much like a nun's habit—a plain, dark blue dress with white collar and cuffs. She must have seen his surprise because she laughed.

'I'm not really a nun, although this is one of the dresses they wear. They decided it would be safer if I wore the same clothes as them so I wouldn't attract too much attention on the way here.'

'I see. But what are you doing in Mwuranda?' he queried.

'Claire is an overseas aid worker,' Kasey explained before the other woman could answer. She shrugged when he glanced at her. 'She was flown out here last year to assess the situation.'

'And you've stayed here all this time?' he asked, turning back to the newcomer because it seemed wiser to focus on her rather than on Kasey. Now that they were back in the office, it was hard not to think about what had happened the other night. He kept getting flashbacks, recalling how it had felt to kiss her, caress her, feel her body pressed against his...

'It wasn't out of choice, I assure you,' Claire replied.

'You mean someone forced you to stay in Mwuranda,' he clarified, trying to steer his thoughts into safer waters. He would drive himself mad if he kept thinking about the other night. It had been a mistake and he should thank his lucky stars that he'd had the sense to stop when he had, but his body was tingling as the memories came flooding back. Kissing Kasey had been the most wonderful experience he'd had in years and there was no point trying to deny it.

'*Something* rather than someone,' Claire corrected, laughing. 'I was meant to fly home once I'd established what kind of aid was needed here. At the time, it looked as though the conflict was over but then there was another coup and rebel forces took control of the airfield. All flights into the country were banned so I ended up staying at the orphanage where I was based. Fortunately, many Mwurandans are very religious people and the rebel fighters have left the nuns alone.'

'I see, although surely you could have flown home on the plane that brought us here?' he suggested.

'I could but I'd have felt as though I was leaving the nuns in the lurch.' She sighed. 'Most of them are very old and frail, I'm afraid. That's why I wanted to see you, in fact. Sister Eleanor fell the other day and broke her hip so I was hoping you might be able to send someone over to see her.'

'Would it be possible to bring her to the hospital?'

'I don't think she'd survive the journey. She doesn't complain, bless her, but she's in a great deal of pain,' Claire explained. 'There are also a lot of children in the orphanage who need treating. They suffered the most terrible injuries during the fighting so if you could spare one of your doctors for a couple of days, it would make a huge difference.'

'If Sister Eleanor has broken her hip, she'll need more than a visit from a doctor. She'll need surgery and proper nursing care afterwards—' Adam began.

'That's where I come in. I'm a qualified nurse so I can look after her. Kasey told me that she'd be willing to help us so now all we need is your blessing… Oh, and a surgeon, of course. That's vital!'

Adam didn't know what to say. He knew he should refuse because they really didn't have enough staff to send a team to the orphanage when they were hard-pressed as it was to keep on top of the work at the hospital. He opened his mouth to explain as gently as he could that it just wasn't possible when Kasey interrupted.

'Please, Adam. I know how pushed we are, but just think of all those children. They desperately need our help, so isn't there anything we can do for them?'

It would have needed a much harder heart than his to withstand the beseeching note in her voice and he sighed. 'All right. I'll see what I can come up with, but I'm not making any promises, you understand?'

'I do. Thank you,' she said, smiling at him so that his heart—which had already been acting oddly—kicked up another storm.

'And thank you from me, too.' Claire held out her hand and he shook it, trying not to think about how wonderful it felt to be on the receiving end of Kasey's smile. It was stupid to let himself get carried away.

Claire asked him for some paper and quickly drew them a map so they would be able to find the orphanage. She left soon after that, obviously eager to go back and tell everyone the good news. Kasey came around the desk and stopped in front of him.

'Thank you again for agreeing to help, Adam.'

'I must be mad to add to our workload,' he said wryly.

'No, you're not mad. You care about people and that's what makes you the person you are.' She touched him lightly on the arm then quickly left the office and he heard her footsteps hurrying along the corridor.

Adam took a deep breath and it felt as though the tension which had had him in its grip for the past couple of days had suddenly melted away. He hadn't realised just how stressful he'd found it to be at loggerheads with her. It simply reinforced his desire to make his peace with her before she went back to England, but would it be possible to do that?

He obviously still had feelings for her because otherwise he wouldn't react the way he did around her, so maybe he needed to decide how he really felt about her and start from there…

His thoughts flicked sideways and his mouth compressed as he hurriedly left the office. Deciding that he was still in love with her wasn't an option!

'You need to turn left just after that burnt-out truck.'

Kasey pointed out the turning then grabbed hold of the door as the Jeep swung round the corner. She checked the map Claire had left them and nodded. 'Yep. This is the right road. She's marked that hotel just here.'

She held out the map so Adam could check for himself that they were going the right way, still finding it hard to believe that he'd asked her to accompany him to the orphanage. She'd expected him to take Daniel but he'd sought her out at dinner the previous night and asked her if she would go with him. It had been a very public olive branch and she'd had no hesitation about accepting it.

Maybe it marked an upturn in their relationship, she thought wistfully, then stamped on the thought before it had time to put down any roots. There was no point setting herself up for a disappointment.

'Take the next turning on the right then straight across at the crossroads...' She paused when she spotted a familiar stretch of road up ahead. 'I came this way the other day when I went to fetch Sarah!'

'Did you?' Adam began to slow down as they approached the intersection.

'No, don't slow down!' she warned him, pointing to the gang of youths on the corner. 'Lester told me it was too dangerous to stop so drive straight across.'

Adam didn't say anything but she saw his hands grip the steering-wheel and had a good idea what he was thinking as they crossed to the other side.

'You need to turn left again just here,' she instructed quietly, knowing that she'd deserved that telling-off he'd given her. Driving on her own had been a crazy thing to do. Not only had she put her life and Lester's at risk but she might have lost the Jeep. There were very few serviceable vehicles in the country and one like this, in good working order, was a highly valuable commodity. It made her see that she owed Adam an apology.

'I'm really sorry about the other day.' She shrugged when he glanced at her. 'I shouldn't have gone off on my own like that. It was a stupid thing to do and you had every right to be angry with me.'

'What's done is done and there's no point harping on about it.' He glanced at the map she was holding. 'Where to now?'

'Left at the end of this road then another left immediately after that.'

She bit her lip when he merely nodded because it was obvious that he didn't intend to discuss what had happened. As far as he was concerned, he'd dealt with the problem and that was that, but it could never be so cut and dried for her. It wasn't just that she'd shown such an appalling lack of judgement, it was what had happened afterwards that was so difficult to deal with. No matter what he'd said at the time, there was no escaping the fact that he'd wanted her and it was hard to understand why he'd felt like that after what had gone on five years ago. Was it possible that Adam still had feelings for her?

The thought hummed away at the back of her mind as they completed their journey. Claire came hurrying out to meet them as soon as they drew up in front of the orphanage, smiling broadly when she saw Kasey.

'Brilliant! I was hoping you'd be able to come. Here, let me take that bag for you.'

'Thanks.' Kasey handed her the case of drugs then picked up a box of instruments from the footwell. 'I wanted to make sure they didn't get broken on the way,' she explained, easing herself out of the seat. 'The roads are so full of potholes that it's impossible to avoid them.'

'Tell me about it.' Claire rolled her eyes. 'I used a moped to get to the hospital the other day. It was like driving on an assault course, picking my way around all the holes in the tarmac!'

Kasey laughed. 'I know what you mean. My backside is probably black and blue from being bounced up and down on that seat!'

'I hope you aren't casting aspersions on my driving skills,' Adam interjected as he came to join them. He grinned at her and her heart caught when she saw the warmth in his eyes. 'I can always make you walk back to the hospital, don't forget, so be very careful what you say!'

'You wouldn't be that cruel,' she said lightly, struggling to keep a rein on her emotions. It was just a smile after all, nothing to get too excited about and yet it felt like a bright spot at the end of a very dark and lonely tunnel.

'Mmm, probably not.'

He treated her to another smile before he turned to follow Claire inside, and Kasey could barely contain her delight. The thought that he had softened enough to tease her made her feel like dancing for joy. Her feet barely seemed to touch the ground as she followed them into the building. Claire led them across a large square entrance hall. Although the place was spotlessly clean, it was very spartan: there were no rugs on the bare wooden floor and no pictures on the walls. Claire stopped outside a door on the far side of the hall and turned to them.

'I'll introduce you to Sister Beatrice first. She's in charge of the orphanage. She's a bit of stickler but don't let that put you off. She's delighted that you've agreed to help us.'

'After the introductions are over, maybe we could see Sister Eleanor,' Adam suggested. 'I'd like to get that hip sorted out as soon as possible.'

'Fine.' Claire tapped on the door and a voice bade them enter. Sister Beatrice was sitting behind an old-fashioned mahogany desk and she stood up when they entered the room. A tall, thin woman dressed in the familiar dark blue dress, she cut an imposing figure.

'Thank you for coming,' she said politely, shaking hands. 'Claire told me that you have agreed to treat Sister Eleanor and take a look at the children.'

'I only wish we could do more to help,' Adam said sincerely. 'Unfortunately, we don't have enough staff to spend very much time here. What I suggest we do is move anyone who needs specialist treatment to the hospital.'

'That seems the most sensible course to me.' She turned to Claire. 'Perhaps you could go with them, my dear. The children know you so it would be less of an ordeal for them if you were there.'

'Of course,' Claire agreed immediately. They exchanged a few more pleasantries before Claire ushered them out. 'Sister Eleanor is in her room. We didn't like to move her because she's in such pain. I'll take you up to see her now.'

She led them along a series of narrow corridors. They passed what must have been classrooms because Kasey could hear children reciting their multiplication tables. They came to the refectory and Claire paused.

'I thought this might be a good place to hold your clinic. We can fetch the kids in here and line them up for you.'

Adam nodded as he looked around the room. 'Looks fine to me. What do you think, Kasey?'

'Yes. Great.' She peered into the room, frowning when she saw the stacks of plastic chairs piled up against the walls. 'How many children are living here at the moment?'

'Over three hundred, and there's more being brought in every day.' Claire sighed when she gasped. 'It's far too many for us to cope with but we don't have a choice, I'm afraid. It was chaos here when the rebel troops rampaged through the town. Whole families were separated so we have no idea how many of the children have lost both their parents.'

'Surely it will reach a point when you can't take any more?' Kasey exclaimed in dismay.

'We reached that point weeks ago. All I can say is thank heavens the supplies are coming through now, otherwise I don't know how we would manage to feed all the kids.'

She didn't add anything else as she led them up the stairs to the second floor but Kasey knew how difficult it must have been for the nuns to look after the children. It simply strengthened her desire to do all she could to help them while they were there. Adam obviously shared her view because he drew her aside while Claire went to tell Sister Eleanor that the doctors would like to examine her.

'As soon as we get back to base, I'm going to see if I can arrange for more supplies to be flown over here.'

'Good idea. They obviously need them, especially if there's going to be an increase in the number of children they're having to care for.'

'We'll sort something out,' he assured her, then broke off when Claire opened the door and invited them into the room.

Sister Eleanor was lying on her bed and it was immediately apparent that she was in a great deal of pain. Adam introduced himself then examined her, and Kasey could tell it wasn't good news.

'I'm afraid the neck of the femur is fractured,' he explained gently. 'That's why you're suffering so much pain in your hip and groin. I'll need to operate and either reduce the fracture and pin the bone together, or replace the entire head and neck of the femur with a plastic one. I can't tell you which method I'll use until I see what state your bones are in.'

'It seems a lot of trouble for you to go to, Dr Chandler,' the elderly nun said worriedly.

'It's no trouble at all.' He patted her hand. 'We'll soon have you back on your feet.'

'I just don't want to be a nuisance—' she began.

'You aren't,' he said firmly turning to Kasey. 'Would you check Sister over while Claire finds me somewhere we can use as a temporary theatre?'

'Of course.'

Kasey went to the bed after he and Claire left and explained what she was going to do. 'I'll be in charge of the anaesthetic when Dr Chandler operates so I need to decide which drugs I should use. I'd like to examine you again if you don't mind, Sister.'

'It seems wrong for you to waste your time on me when so many of the children need your help, Dr Harris,' Sister Eleanor protested weakly.

Kasey shook her head. 'It isn't a waste of time because once you are well again, you'll be able to help look after the children, won't you?'

That seemed to reassure the elderly woman and she didn't protest any more when Kasey took out her stethoscope. She checked Sister Eleanor's heart, lungs and circulation and wasn't at all happy with her findings. The nun had a chest infection and that could prove a problem if she was given a general anaesthetic. When Adam came back, she took him outside so she could explain her findings to him.

'I'm not happy about giving her a general anaesthetic. There's definite signs of a chest infection and it's far too risky.'

'So what do you suggest?'

'A spinal block. I can keep her just under the surface—not in pain but aware of what's happening. I'll also put in a catheter so Claire can top up her pain relief after we've left.'

'Fine. I'm happy to leave it to you.'

'Thanks. Did you find somewhere suitable to use as a theatre?'

'Yes. They have a small sick-bay, which will do. It's light and clean and that's all we need, basically.'

She grinned. 'Don't let your hospital manager back home know you said that or he will start making budget cuts. I remember the fights you had to get decent funding when I worked at St Edward's.'

'Don't remind me!' He raised his eyes. 'It felt as though I was beating my head against a brick wall most of the time. And they were such piffling little things I was asking for, too—new scrub suits for the staff, decent drapes, theatres to be cleaned every time they were used and not just once a day. All basic necessities yet you'd have thought I was asking for the moon.'

She chuckled. 'I know. But you won most of the battles. Not many people were willing to get in your way when you were on the warpath, Adam. You had the staff jumping through hoops to make sure they did what you wanted them to do.'

'All except you. I don't remember you jumping through any hoops to please me, Kasey. You stood your ground from the moment we met, as I recall.'

'Oh, I was quaking in my boots as well even if I didn't show it,' she retorted.

'Really?' He frowned. 'I never realised I was such a hard taskmaster.'

'You're so completely focused on your job that you probably don't realise the effect you have on the people around you.'

'That's true.'

He took a deep breath yet his voice seemed to grate all of a sudden so that Kasey felt herself tense.

'I certainly didn't realise the effect I had on your brother.'

CHAPTER SIX

ADAM watched myriad expressions cross Kasey's face and wished with all of his heart that he'd never said that.

What was the point of raking it all up again? It wouldn't change what had happened so why had he felt the need to…to *justify* himself. Did he really think it would make everything right between them?

'You mean, it never crossed your mind that telling a young doctor he wasn't cut out for medicine would have repercussions?' She laughed scornfully. 'I find that very hard to believe!'

'I hoped it would encourage him to get his act together,' he said gruffly. 'You don't have any idea what the background was to that conversation.'

'I know what Keiran told me—that you did nothing but criticise him from the moment he set foot in your department. You found fault with every single thing he did until you wore him down. That's why he left medicine and *that's* why he ended up making such a mess of his life!'

She swung round before he could reply and marched down the stairs. Adam took a deep breath but it was painful to know that she still blamed him for her brother's problems. He could tell her the truth, of course, but would she believe him, or would she think he was making it up to try and offset the blame from himself?

It was impossible to decide. He needed to think it all through before he did anything, not least because Kasey would be terribly hurt when she found out what had really gone on. Obviously, Keiran hadn't told her everything; he'd been highly selective. He hadn't told her about the number of times he hadn't shown up for work, or about the times he'd arrived in no fit state to be allowed near the patients.

Adam knew that he'd had to lay down the law to avoid a disaster but explaining that to Kasey was another matter. It was why he hadn't told her five years ago—the thought of adding to her distress by shattering the image she'd had of her brother had been more than he could bear, and it was no easier now. He decided to wait before he said anything and made his way to the sick-bay. Kasey was already there, getting everything ready, and his heart ached when he saw how strained she looked.

'The light is better by the window so I'll move this table over there. It will have to serve as an operating table,' he told her. He positioned the table close to the window and covered it with a sterile drape from the box of supplies they'd brought with them.

'Excuse me.'

Kasey stepped around him and placed the drip stand at one end of the table. She hung a bag of saline on it and placed a catheter—still in its pack—on the end of the table. Adam frowned as he watched her fetch the other items she needed—a fine-bore needle, swabs, some antiseptic wipes as well as the drugs she would use.

'You need something to put your equipment on,' he decided, looking around.

'There's a cabinet in the bathroom,' she told him shortly, turning towards a door he hadn't noticed before.

'I'll get it,' he offered immediately, but she ignored him as she went into the bathroom. She reappeared a few seconds later with the cabinet and this time he didn't make the mistake of trying to help. She didn't want his help, as she was making it abundantly clear.

The thought was more depressing than it should have been. Adam's mouth thinned as he went to fetch Sister

Eleanor. He couldn't help wishing that he'd asked Daniel to accompany him to the orphanage. He'd hoped to smooth things over by taking Kasey along on the visit, but it wasn't working out that way.

So much for hoping to make his peace with her. There was too much back history between them so maybe he should just get everything out into the open—tell her the truth about her brother and be done with it—but it wasn't going to be easy. No matter what she'd done to him in the past, he didn't want to hurt her.

The operation to repair Sister Eleanor's hip went very smoothly, considering the lack of any proper facilities. Adam was able to repair the hip by pinning and plating the neck of the femur together. Kasey had opted for the spinal block—injecting a small amount of the anaesthetic agent into the cerebrospinal fluid in the lumbar spine region.

She chose the site of the injection with care because if it was too high up the respiratory system could be compromised. Because blocking the nerves in any area could result in hypotension—low blood pressure—she monitored the patient very carefully, but there were no problems. Claire had offered to assist them and proved invaluable as she acted as their theatre nurse. Kasey could tell that Adam was pleased as he finished putting in the final suture.

'Excellent!' he declared. 'It couldn't have gone any better if we'd been in a real theatre.'

'Just shows what you can do with a bit of imagination,' Claire said cheerfully, gathering up the instruments they'd used. She took them into the bathroom as Adam turned to Kasey.

'We may as well leave Sister Eleanor in here. There's no point trying to move her back to her room when there's a perfectly good bed available here.'

'That seems the most sensible option,' she agreed, doing her best to match his tone. Now that the pressure of the operation was off, she could feel herself getting all steamed up again. Adam's refusal to accept that he'd treated her brother in a very cavalier fashion had really hurt. She'd hoped that he might have seen the error of his ways by now, but he'd made it clear that he didn't think he'd been in the wrong. Now all the doubts she'd had about whether he really was to blame had suddenly disappeared.

It was *his* fault that Keiran had gone off the rails, and *his* fault, too, that her brother had abandoned his career. If Adam weren't so full of his own importance, he would have realised the damage he'd caused!

She stood up abruptly, knowing that she couldn't sit there, bottling up her anger, or she would explode and she didn't want to have a row with him in public. 'I'll have a word with Claire and see if one of the nuns can look after Sister Eleanor while we see to the children.'

'Good idea. I'll leave you to sort things out while I get everything set up in the dining room.' He took his watch out of his pocket and frowned. 'It's almost eleven o'clock already and we still have loads to do. I really want to head back before it starts getting dark.'

'We'd better get a move on, then,' Kasey said shortly. She went into the bathroom where Claire was washing the instruments they'd used. She glanced round when Kasey appeared.

'I'll pack these up ready for you to sterilise them when you get back to the hospital.'

'Thanks. That would be a help. Adam has suggested that we leave Sister Eleanor in the sick-bay rather than move her back upstairs. Could one of the other nuns sit with her while we take a look at the children, do you think?'

'Of course. I'll sort out a rota so there's someone with

her at all times,' Claire assured her, drying her hands. 'How is she?'

'A bit groggy but she should be fine in an hour or so. I'm going to leave the catheter in so you'll be able to administer pain relief whenever she needs it. It will be far more effective that way so long as you're happy to take charge of it.'

'No problem. I did it umpteen times when I was a ward sister.'

'What made you decide to leave nursing?' Kasey asked curiously.

'Oh, a general feeling of disillusionment and a desire to do something positive with my life—the usual story,' Claire said lightly.

Kasey sensed there was more to the tale but she didn't press her for any details. Everyone had secrets, herself and Adam included. She sighed because every thought ended up back with him. Drawing that line under the past wasn't proving an easy thing to do.

Once Sister Eleanor was comfortably settled she headed for the dining room and found that Adam had everything prepared. He'd arranged a table and a couple of chairs on each side of the room for them to work from. He'd also laid out all the usual paraphernalia they would need— stethoscopes and rubber gloves, tongue depressors, etcetera. He looked round when she went into the room.

'Good timing. I was just about to make a start. One of the nuns has gone to fetch the first lot of children. She's going to bring the youngest ones through first.'

'Anything in particular that I should look out for?' Kasey asked politely.

'I'd guess malnutrition will be one of the problems we'll see today. A lot of children in developing countries suffer from kwashiorkor or marasmus.'

'So what are the symptoms?'

'A child with kwashiorkor will have a greatly distended abdomen, stunted growth and a puffy appearance caused by oedema. He may be apathetic and irritable, and often his skin will flake off, leaving raw patches,' he explained, sitting on the edge of the desk. 'The hair can be very brittle and it often changes colour and becomes much lighter. Oh, and the liver may be enlarged, too.'

'And marasmus,' she asked rather faintly.

'Similar cause, i.e. an inadequate intake of protein and calories, but the kids are usually emaciated with folds of loose skin on their limbs and buttocks.'

'And the solution... There is a solution, I hope?'

'Yes. Depending on how ill the child is, he should recover with an adequate diet. High-protein, high-energy foods are vital.'

'Can the orphanage provide the children with that kind of a diet, though?' she asked worriedly. 'They're over-stretched as it is.'

'That's the worrying part, but I'll get in touch with the agency as soon as we return to base and organise something.' He straightened when the sound of voices in the corridor announced that the first group of children had arrived. 'Just do your best, Kasey. It's all any of us can do.'

He gave her a quick smile before he walked over to one of the tables and sat down. Kasey took her own seat, praying that she would be able to cope. She'd never done this type of work before and only hoped she wouldn't let him down...

She frowned when it struck her how important it was not to disappoint him. Bearing in mind everything that had gone on today, it shouldn't have mattered but it did. She didn't want Adam thinking badly of her—for any reason.

Her heart contracted as she glanced across the room. There was no point pretending that she didn't care what he thought. Adam's opinion had mattered to her in the

past, too, strangely enough. She'd wanted him to like her
then, and not just because of Keiran and the plans she'd
made, and it was exactly the same now. She hated it when
they continually argued yet she couldn't understand why
she felt this strongly.

Well, there was no point worrying about it when she'd
be leaving in a week or so's time. That Adam would be
glad to see the back of her wasn't in question!

The next few hours flew past. Some of the children were
excited about being seen by a doctor, others were scared
and some were just so traumatised by what they'd experienced that they didn't care. Kasey lost count of the number who were suffering from malnutrition. Most of the
children had been living on scraps for years and their
health had deteriorated badly.

A lot of them had worms, too, so she told the nuns who
were helping her that she would give them medication to
treat all the children in the orphanage. Several of the older
boys had quite severe injuries—one had lost a hand after
a land-mine had exploded when he'd picked it up and another a leg—so she sent them to Adam because he would
be able to assess what could be done for them far better
than her. One little three-year-old boy called Kofi had a
paralysed lower left arm. The muscles in both his hand
and his forearm were so badly wasted that his fingers were
curved inwards like a claw. Kasey took him over to Adam
to see if he knew what was wrong with him.

'Looks like Klumpke's paralysis.' Adam gently rotated
the boy's arm and nodded. 'Yes. That's what it is. The
first thoracic nerve in the brachial plexus has been damaged.'

'The network of nerves behind the shoulder blade? Do
you think his shoulder was dislocated at some point and
that's how it was damaged?'

'Probably when he was born. It's the most common cause of this type of injury.' He smiled at the child. 'I might be able to make your arm feel a bit better, Kofi, so will you wait over there for me?' He ruffled the child's hair when he nodded solemnly. 'Good boy!'

He turned to Kasey as the child obediently moved away. 'I might be able to do something to help him regain a little more mobility. Exercises might help to strengthen his arm, although there isn't much I can do about the damage to the nerve, I'm afraid.'

'Anything would be better than nothing,' she assured him, then turned away because she didn't want him to see how moved she was by the way he'd treated the child.

He'd always had a wonderful way with his patients, treating them with a gentle authority that had immediately allayed their fears. It was a side of him she'd always admired, in fact. Adam might be a stickler when it came to his staff but he'd never had any difficulty relating to his patients and it was unsettling to be reminded of that fact.

They carried on for another hour but it was obvious that they wouldn't be able to see all the children that day. When Claire came to check how she was doing, Kasey grimaced.

'Not too well, I'm afraid. There's too many who need more than just a basic health check. We'll never be able to get through them all today.'

'Maybe you could stay the night and see the rest tomorrow,' Claire suggested hopefully.

'I'm perfectly happy to stay but I'm not sure if Adam will agree so maybe you should check with him. I know he was planning on driving back to the hospital.'

'At this time of the day?' Claire pulled a face as she glanced out of the window. 'It will be dark soon so it sounds a bit risky to me, but I'll see what he says.'

Kasey packed everything away, apart from her notes.

Several of the children needed medication and she wanted to have a word with Claire about the best way to organise their treatment. She glanced up when a shadow fell over her and felt her heart squeeze in an extra beat when she saw Adam standing by the table. Maybe it was that reminder about the way he'd behaved so sympathetically towards his patients but all of a sudden she felt incredibly shy with him.

'Did Claire ask you about spending the night here?' she said quickly, because she didn't want him to think there was anything wrong. He hadn't treated Keiran with sympathy, she reminded herself, yet for some reason it was difficult to relate the man she'd seen that afternoon to the person who had ruined her brother's life. Was it really possible for someone to exhibit two such opposing sides to his character?

'Yes. I must admit that I hadn't planned on staying but it would solve a few problems. We've only seen about half the children so far and I'd feel happier if we could see the rest before we left. Plus I don't fancy having to drive back to the hospital in the dark. How do you feel about staying the night here, though?'

'I don't mind. I'm happy to stay if you think it would be the best thing to do,' she agreed hurriedly, not wanting to dwell on such disquieting thoughts because they only confused the issue.

'I do actually. Right, that's agreed, then. We'll stay the night and see the rest of the kids in the morning then drive back after lunch.'

'Fine by me, although I wish I'd brought a change of clothes with me,' she said ruefully, glancing down at the once-white T-shirt she was wearing. Lots of sticky little hands had left their marks and she felt grubby and sweaty and in dire need of something clean to wear.

'Have a word with Claire and see if she can lend you

something,' he suggested, then grinned. 'Somehow, I don't think the good sisters will have anything to fit me, though, so I'll just make do with what I've got on.'

Kasey chuckled. 'I can't quite see you in one of their dresses…'

'Not quite my thing,' he agreed dryly, then glanced round when Claire came back to tell them that she'd spoken to Sister Beatrice who had offered to let them sleep in the annexe.

Claire took them to see it, explaining on the way that it was normally used by the local priest when he visited the orphanage and that was why it had been built onto the side of the chapel. She unlocked the door and showed them around, not that there was much to see. There were just three rooms in all—a small bedroom with an iron-framed bed, a sitting room with a sofa that converted into a second bed and a bathroom. There was no kitchen because Father Michael always ate with the nuns when he was there, but it was more than adequate for their needs.

Claire immediately offered to lend her some clothes when Kasey mentioned her dilemma. She hurried away to find something suitable for her then Adam announced that he was going back to the orphanage to start compiling a list of the children who would need to be seen at the hospital.

Kasey decided to make the most of having the place to herself and took a bath. Mindful of the need to conserve water, she filled the tub only part way but it felt wonderful to wash off the grime. She washed her hair with a bar of soap she found in the dish then got out and wrapped a towel around herself. The thought of having to put her dirty clothes back on was more than she could face so she heaved a sigh of relief when she heard someone coming into the annexe because it meant that Claire must have brought her something clean to wear.

Opening the bathroom door, she hurried out to meet her and stopped dead when she discovered that it wasn't Claire who'd come in but Adam. Her heart gave an almighty lurch when she saw his eyes travel over her before they swiftly returned to her face. All she had on was the damp towel and she was very conscious of the fact that it did little to conceal her modesty.

'I thought you were Claire,' she said, her tongue sticking to the roof of her mouth in embarrassment. 'She promised to bring me some clean clothes.'

'She wanted to check on Sister Eleanor so she asked me to give them to you.' Adam's expression was unreadable as he motioned towards a pile of clothes neatly stacked on the end of the couch.

'Oh. Right. Thank you.'

Kasey knew that she should collect the clothes and beat a hasty retreat, but she was a bit wary about letting go of the towel while she picked them up. Maybe Adam realised her predicament because he picked up the bundle.

'I'll put them in the bedroom for you.'

'Thanks.' She stepped out of the way so he could get past her then cried out in alarm when her feet suddenly skidded on the tiled floor.

'Careful!' Adam dropped the bundle of clothing as he grabbed hold of her arm and hauled her upright again.

'Oh! I don't know how that happened,' she exclaimed shakily. 'My feet just skidded out from under me.'

'It's no damned wonder when you're dripping wet. You should have had more sense than to go parading around in that state.'

Kasey flushed at the unwarranted rebuke. 'I apologise,' she said stiffly, easing her arm out of his grasp. 'Next time I'll be more careful.'

Adam didn't say anything as he picked up the clothes and took them into the bedroom. He dropped them onto the bed then headed back out of the room, barely glancing at her as he made his way to the door.

'Claire said to tell you that dinner is at six. Apparently, Sister Beatrice takes a dim view of anyone being late.'

'I'll be there on time,' Kasey assured him, although it was doubtful if he'd heard her because he was already on his way out of the door.

She went into the bedroom after he'd left, making sure the door was securely closed before she removed the towel. There was no way she wanted him coming back and finding her naked. She'd had the distinct impression that he thought she had deliberately gone out to meet him wearing nothing more than a towel, but he couldn't have been more wrong.

Her lips compressed as she sorted a clean pair of cotton panties out of the pile of clothing and stepped into them. There was no danger of her trying to seduce him if that was what he feared. She wasn't about to make her life even more complicated than it already was!

Adam made his way along the path, only stopping when he reached the fence that marked the boundary of the grounds. The orphanage had been built on the very edge of the town and beyond it lay only scrubland. There were no lights to be seen apart from a few early evening stars and no distractions from his thoughts, which was what he wanted. He needed to apply the same ruthless determination to ridding his mind of these images as he applied to everything else.

He took a deep breath and made himself remember what he'd seen: alabaster-pale skin glistening with moisture; long, wet strands of black hair curling around a delicate oval face; damp cotton towelling clinging to lush curves…

He groaned as a dozen different emotions hit him all at once. How he'd managed to let Kasey go just now was beyond him. It had taken every scrap of willpower he'd possessed not to haul her into his arms, strip off that damned towel and take her right there and then on the floor. After all, that was what she'd been angling for, wasn't it? Why else had she appeared wearing nothing more than that flimsy scrap of cotton? Maybe she'd claimed that she'd thought he was Claire but why should he believe her? It certainly wasn't the first time that she'd set out to seduce him…

He cut off that thought in mid-flight, unable to bear any more. Remembering what a fool he'd been in the past wasn't going to help him at the moment. He had no idea what she was up to but she was definitely planning something. Maybe she thought she could persuade him to let her stay in Mwuranda by using the oldest trick in the book, but it wasn't going to work. As soon as he could get her on a plane home, she was leaving!

He felt a bit better after re-confirming his decision to send her back to England. Somewhere during the day he'd started to wonder if he was being a bit too hard on her but now he was sure he was doing the right thing. Life would return to some sort of normality once Kasey left, and he just needed to hang onto that thought.

He made his way back to the orphanage and continued working on his notes, only breaking off when the children began to arrive for dinner. Tucking the papers into his briefcase, he moved out of the way as they trooped in. It was all very orderly and he sighed as he watched them quietly collect their plates and make their way to their seats. There was no pushing or shoving, certainly none of the usual fun and games one might have expected to see with such a large group of children. When you'd nearly starved to death, eating became a serious business.

'Do they ever really get over it, do you think?'

He glanced round when he heard Kasey's voice beside

him. 'Get over what?' he asked, playing for time because he wasn't sure he could hold up his end of a conversation while his heart was beating at this tempo. She was wearing some of the clothes Claire had lent her—a long-sleeved blue blouse with a pair of worn denim jeans—so there was no excuse for the way he was behaving at the moment.

This outfit definitely wasn't pulling gear! The best that could be said for it was that it was clean and serviceable, so why on earth was he so aroused by the sight of her? Was it the fact that her skin seemed to glow with a pearly sheen in the lamplight, or because her hair smelt so sweetly of soap? There had to be a reason why his body was behaving this way but, try as he would, he couldn't think what it was. The last time he'd laid the blame very firmly at her door—flaunting herself in that towel had been more temptation than any red-blooded male could be expected to withstand. But dressed in sensible jeans and blouse...?

Adam began to sweat. He could feel the moisture beading on his upper lip, trickling between his shoulder blades, feel his palms growing damp. There was no excuse for his behaviour now so all he could do was face up to the truth. Kasey wouldn't need to seduce him this time any more than she'd needed to seduce him the last time. He'd been desperate to sleep with her five years ago and he was desperate to sleep with her again now. Not even the long, lonely years of regret had cured him of this affliction so where did he go from here? Did he give in and admit that he wanted her? Or should he hold fast?

He groaned deep in his throat. Whichever decision he made, it looked as though he was in for a really rough time tonight!

CHAPTER SEVEN

KASEY frowned when she heard Adam groan. She glanced at him and was shocked to see what looked very much like panic on his face.

'Are you feeling all right?' she asked in concern.

'Fine. Never better. Come along. We're keeping everyone waiting.'

A large hand suddenly clamped itself around her elbow as he whisked her towards the top table where Sister Beatrice was waiting to greet them. Kasey summoned a smile as the elderly woman invited them to sit beside her, but she had to admit that she was a little confused by his behaviour. One of the nuns placed a plate in front of her and she thanked her, but she seemed to be functioning on two separate levels. What on earth was the matter with him?

Sister Beatrice clapped her hands and everyone stood while she said grace. They sat down and Kasey picked up her fork and dug into the spicy bean concoction they'd been served.

'The answer is no.'

She looked up when Adam spoke to her. 'No what?' she repeated blankly.

'You asked if the children ever really get over what they've been through.' He shrugged. 'In my experience they never do. They've suffered too much for it not to have left scars on them.'

'That's what I thought,' she said quietly.

'The best we can do is arrange for them to receive counselling. We have a psychiatrist who works for us so maybe he can put together a team of volunteers to come out here and talk to the children.'

'Their needs must be somewhat different to those of the people Worlds Together normally helps, though.'

She stirred the stew with her fork, wondering why he seemed so eager to talk all of a sudden. She'd expected him to cut her dead after what had happened earlier that evening, but he seemed very keen to discuss the problems the children faced.

'That's very true. Normally we treat people in the aftermath of a natural disaster. Obviously, they're traumatised by what they've been through but there's a kind of acceptance because what happened was beyond their control. It's very different in this instance.'

'There must be people who are trained to deal with this type of situation, though,' she suggested, doing her best to keep the conversation rolling because she sensed it was what he wanted.

'I'm sure there are. The armed services have counsellors so maybe we can get some help from them. They would know all about the problems specific to people who've been living in a war zone.'

Kasey nodded, wishing she could think of something erudite to say on the matter but she knew too little about the subject to contribute very much to the conversation. Fortunately, Adam didn't seem deterred by her silence as he continued in the same, rather evangelical tone.

'These kids have seen sights most adults couldn't cope with so they'll definitely need skilled people to counsel them. I'll get in touch with Shiloh and see what can be arranged.'

'Good idea,' she agreed, then looked round in relief when Sister Beatrice asked her how Sister Eleanor was faring.

Kasey explained that the operation had been a success

and that it shouldn't be long before Sister Eleanor was up and about again, but it was difficult to concentrate when she was so aware of Adam sitting beside her.

She shot a glance his way and frowned when she saw the strained expression on his face. He looked really on edge and she couldn't understand what was wrong with him. He'd seemed very much in control when he'd berated her for parading around the annexe earlier that evening, so what had happened in the interim?

By the time dinner ended, she was a bundle of nerves and wasn't looking forward to having to go back to the annexe and spend the evening making polite conversation with him. When Claire asked her if she wanted to join her for a cup of coffee, she eagerly agreed.

'I'd love to!' she exclaimed, standing up. The nuns had already ushered the children out of the dining room so there were just the three of them left. She held her breath when Claire asked Adam if he would like to join them because she really could do with a breathing space away from him.

'Thanks, but I think I'll go back to the annexe and finish off that list I was compiling,' he explained, picking up his briefcase. 'We're bound to see more children tomorrow who will need to be hospitalised and it will save time if I've done most of the paperwork tonight.'

'Do you want me to give you a hand?' Kasey offered, feeling guilty about leaving him to do all the work.

'No, it's fine. You go and have a coffee with Claire.'

'Right.' Kasey didn't argue as she followed Claire out of the dining room. They went straight to the kitchen where Claire filled a huge, soot-blackened kettle with water and placed it on the hob.

'It will take a while to boil because it's a wood-burning stove,' Claire warned her, taking a couple of thick white mugs off a shelf.

'No problem. I'm certainly not in any rush to go back to the annexe.'

Claire arched a brow. 'Why? Has something happened?'

'No, of course not...' she began, then sighed, because there was no point pretending everything was fine. 'Adam's been acting very strangely since he caught me parading around in a towel earlier on tonight.'

'I see.' Claire chuckled. 'I thought he looked a bit up-tight during dinner.'

'You noticed it, too?' She plonked herself down on a chair. 'He obviously believes I did it on purpose but it was just an accident!'

'And now you're worried in case he thinks he might be in for a night of passion?' Claire grinned as she took a jar of instant coffee out of a cupboard. 'Would that be such a dreadful thing? I mean, he is rather gorgeous, isn't he?'

'He is, but it's not that simple. He and I...well, we used to be an item at one time.'

'Really?' Claire spooned some coffee into the mugs then sat down opposite her. 'So what happened? Did you break it off? Did he? Or was it all some terrible misunderstanding and you've been pining away for love of one another ever since?' She gave a theatrically wistful sigh and Kasey laughed.

'The answer is no to all of those!'

'Then what did happen?' Claire sobered abruptly. 'If it would help to talk about it, Kasey, I swear that anything you tell me won't go any further.'

'It's kind of you, Claire, but it's very complicated.'

'Affairs of the heart usually are,' Claire said flatly.

'Yes, I expect so, but this was even more complicated than most...' Kasey bit her lip but the urge to tell someone about what had happened was suddenly too strong to resist. 'It wasn't just a question of Adam and I being attracted to each other, you see. I...well, I deliberately set out to make him fall for me, to pay him back for what he did to my brother.'

'Wow! You weren't kidding when you said it was complicated.' Claire sat back in her seat and stared at her in amazement. 'I take it that your plan worked?'

'Oh, yes. Only too well.' Kasey laughed shortly. 'I'd covered every angle from getting myself a job at the hospital where Adam worked to *accidentally* bumping into him the day I arrived. Nobody could have planned it better, if I say so myself.'

'And did it turn out how you'd envisaged it would?'

'No, not really. I'd just meant to shake him up a bit, make him see how it felt to lose something you thought was important to you, but it got out of hand. He…well, I think he really loved me.'

'I see. And how did you feel about him?'

'The same.' She smiled sadly. 'It was the one thing I hadn't allowed for. I didn't want to fall in love with him, believe me, because he'd destroyed Keiran's life, but I just couldn't stop myself. I fell head over heels in love with him and there was nothing I could do about it.'

'And don't you find that just a little bit strange?'

'What do you mean?'

Claire shrugged. 'You just said that you didn't want to fall in love with Adam because of what he'd done, so why did you? What attracted you to him?'

'Oh, I don't know…'

'Yes, you do. Think about it.'

'His looks…the way he behaved towards me,' she said slowly. 'The fact that he was so dedicated to his job and how he was with the patients—always kind, never testy like some surgeons are. He was also such good company…witty, fun, charming, considerate…'

She stopped abruptly, shocked to have found so many good points to list.

'In other words, he was nothing like you expected him to be?'

Kasey shook her head because there was a lump the size of Africa suddenly lodged in her throat. She had a horrible feeling that she knew what Claire was going to say next but she couldn't stop her.

'Then do you think you could have been wrong about him, Kasey? Is it possible that he didn't do all the awful things you thought he'd done? I don't know how it could have happened but it seems to me that you might have made a mistake.'

'A mistake?'

'Yes. Oh, I understand how hard it must be for you to face that fact because I made a mistake myself a few years ago. I believed that the man I loved was in love with me when he was merely stringing me along. Looking back, I suppose I always sensed something wasn't quite right about our relationship but I didn't want to admit it at the time. Maybe the same thing applies in this instance and Adam *wasn't* to blame for what happened to your brother, but you don't want to have to face up to it. It's worth considering, surely?'

Claire didn't say anything else as she got up and made the coffee. Kasey was glad, because she didn't think she could have absorbed anything else. Claire's comments had only reinforced her own doubts, hadn't they? And yet Adam had admitted only that day that he'd told Keiran he wasn't cut out for medicine, so how could she have been mistaken about him?

Her thoughts twisted this way and that so that her head was aching by the time they finished their coffee. She said goodnight to Claire but the thought of going back to the annexe and seeing Adam again while she was so confused was more than she could bear.

She left the main building and followed the path until

she came to an arbour formed by the boughs of a baobab tree. There was a wooden bench inside it and she sat down. It was wonderfully peaceful there with only the night-time sounds to disturb the silence and after a few moments she closed her eyes. She just needed some time on her own to think…

Adam paced the floor. It was ten minutes past midnight and there was still no sign of Kasey. What the hell was she up to? Didn't she realise that they would have to be up really early in the morning if they were to see the rest of the children before they left? She should be trying to get some sleep instead of wasting the night gossiping with Claire!

He let himself out of the annexe and went back to the orphanage but the place was in darkness when he got there. He tried the front door but it was locked. It left him in a bit of a quandary because he had no way of knowing what had happened to Kasey. She could have decided to spend the night in the main building rather than return to the annexe, but surely she would have let him know if there'd been any change to her plans…

Unless she hadn't wanted him to know what she was planning in case he tried to stop her?

Adam's heart began to thump as he raced around to the front of the building. He knew he'd been behaving very strangely that night and that Kasey had noticed it, but surely she hadn't been so alarmed that she'd decided to drive herself back to the hospital? His heart thumped even harder as he ran down the path. He would never forgive himself if anything happened to her!

He rounded the side of the building and ground to a halt when he saw that the Jeep was still parked where he'd left it. Obviously she hadn't left the orphanage so where was she? He was loath to create a scene by hammering on the door and waking everyone up so he decided to eliminate all other possibilities before raising the alarm, starting with a thorough search of the grounds.

He retraced his tracks, following the path until he came to the arbour, and breathed a sigh of relief when he found her fast asleep on the bench. She looked so beautiful as she lay there with her cheek cradled on her hand that he couldn't bear to wake her.

Sitting down on the bench, he stared across the night-darkened garden while he listened to the gentle rhythm of her breathing. It was a sound that filled him with sadness all of a sudden because it reminded him of all the other nights when he'd lain awake listening to her sleeping beside him. Those few, short weeks they'd had together had been the most wonderful time of his entire life. He had never felt so in tune with anyone before, never experienced such closeness as he had with Kasey. Their minds had meshed as perfectly as their bodies and the thought was so sharp, so bitter, that he drew in a ragged breath as pain speared through him. He would never love anyone the way he'd loved Kasey.

'Adam?'

Her voice was husky with the remnants of sleep, and the pain inside him seemed to swell until it consumed him totally. He made himself breathe in then out before he turned to look at her because he wanted, *needed* to be in control of his emotions, yet even so he felt his heart jerk in helpless response when he saw the concern in her beautiful blue eyes. She was concerned about *him* and the thought almost made him keel over, only he couldn't—wouldn't—make a fool of himself again over her.

'Are you all right?'

'I'm fine,' he ground out testily, because gentleness would have been his undoing. But, oddly enough, she didn't round on him as she had the right to do.

Reaching out, she laid her hand on his arm and he had to breathe deeply when he felt the warmth of her fingers seeping into his skin. 'Are you sure? You've been acting very strangely tonight.'

'Have I?' He shrugged, hoping to dislodge her hand, praying that he wouldn't. 'I apologise.'

'Don't be silly.' She huffed out a sigh and his teeth clenched when he felt the sweetness of her breath cloud on his cheek. 'There's no need to apologise. I was just worried in case I'd done something to upset you...'

She broke off and he could tell that she was trying to decide if she should carry on or stop there. All of a sudden, he knew that he didn't want to hear anything else. It wouldn't help and it certainly wouldn't ease this ache in his heart that was rapidly spreading throughout his body. He opened his mouth to tell her that, only she beat him to it.

'I really and truly didn't know it was you coming into the annexe earlier. I thought it was Claire—'

'Forget it.'

He shot to his feet because he couldn't take any more. Getting involved in a discussion about what had happened earlier that evening wouldn't help one bit. He really didn't need to be reminded about how she'd looked when he'd gone back to the annexe...

Alabster skin beaded with moisture.

Long, wet strands of hair falling around her beautiful face.

Lusciously feminine curves imprinted on a damp towel.

The images roared through his head and he cursed softly. Kasey rose to her feet, her face looking pale in the starlight. 'Adam? What is it? What's wrong?'

'Nothing. It's time we went to bed,' he said harshly. 'We have an early start in the morning, don't forget.'

'Is that why you came to find me?' she questioned, and

he saw what looked very much like disappointment in her eyes.

'Yes.'

He turned and led the way up the path because he refused to fall into the trap of trying to second-guess what she was thinking. Nobody could read someone else's thoughts and he certainly couldn't read Kasey's, otherwise he wouldn't be in this situation, would he? He would have realised five years ago that her feelings for him hadn't been genuine and the thought stung. He hated to be made to feel like a fool.

'What were you doing outside anyway?' he snapped like a headmaster carpeting an unruly pupil.

'I wanted some time on my own to think,' she replied with a calmness that only served to highlight his testiness.

Adam struggled to match her tone because he didn't want it to appear as though he was being unreasonable. 'There was a lot to take in today.'

'There was, but it wasn't just work I was thinking about. I needed time to think about what happened. Between us.'

'Let's not go down that road again,' he said brusquely, his resolve immediately fading. The last thing he wanted was to get into another argument while he was in this state of mind. 'So far as I'm concerned, it's all over and done with.'

'Is it?' She followed him into the annexe and her face was set when he turned to look at her. 'I don't see how it can be over until we've talked about what went on.'

'What's there to talk about? I ruined your brother's life. You paid me back. End of story.' His laughter was harsh but he couldn't disguise the pain it held and he saw her flinch.

'And what if I was wrong? What if you weren't to blame? What if I made a terrible mistake?' She took a step towards him and he could see the anguish in her eyes. 'What should I do then, Adam?'

'I can't answer that question,' he said flatly, because if this was some sort of a game she'd dreamed up to torment him, he refused to take part. 'It isn't up to me to tell you what to do, Kasey, as you've pointed out more times than I can count.'

'All right. Maybe you can't tell me what I should do but you can tell me the truth.'

'Why? What possible difference would it make now?' He rounded on her, pain and anger combining into a potent force. 'Our relationship was a sham from start to finish so what's the point of all these questions?'

'The point is that I need to know if I was right about you!'

'Oh, I see. And what if I tell you that you were wrong? Are you going to believe me? Or will you just think I'm lying?'

'I don't know! That's why I need to hear your version of events!' She took a quick breath and her voice was much quieter when she continued. 'I just want to know the truth, Adam. That's all I'm asking.'

'Fine, but you're not going to like it, I warn you.'

He went over to the window, wondering if he was mad to agree. It certainly wouldn't make *him* feel better to shatter those illusions she still had about her brother.

'That's something I'll just have to risk. But I need to know what really went on between you and Keiran, and you are the only person who can tell me. So will you? Please?'

The pleading note in her voice was almost his undoing and he swallowed. He knew how difficult this was going to be for her but maybe it was time she found out the facts. His tone was deliberately bland when he began because he wanted to spare her as much heartache as possible.

'Your brother caused problems from the moment he set foot in the surgical department. I'd been warned what to expect but I hadn't realised how bad the situation really was.'

'Warned? By whom?'

'By his previous departmental head. Keiran had done a stint in Paeds on his previous rotation and he'd been given an official warning about his behaviour while he was there.'

'So your view of him was biased before he even started,' she scoffed. 'You know as well as I do that some people just don't gel—'

'He'd failed to turn up for ward rounds three days in a row so it was a bit more serious than him not gelling with the head of the paediatric team.'

'Maybe he was sick. He told me that he'd not been well—'

'He was drunk, not ill. Too drunk to get out of bed and go to work.'

'That's ridiculous! Keiran doesn't drink. He never drank!'

'And he never took drugs either?'

She flushed at the acerbic note in his voice. 'He got himself into that state because he was working so hard. You know what it's like when you're studying for exams. He was working right through the night and he started taking those pills to help him stay awake.'

'Then needed something else to make him sleep.' He sighed wearily. 'Yes, I know how hard it is, and Keiran wasn't the first student to make that mistake. But he continued taking uppers and downers after he'd finished his exams. He was still taking them while he was doing his rotations.'

'No! He wouldn't have done that. He wouldn't have been so stupid!'

'He was.' Adam held up his hand because it was hard enough to lay out the facts without them having a row as well. 'I know he was taking them, Kasey, because I caught him popping pills one day in the staffroom. I told him then that he had to clean up his act or he would be out on his ear.'

'And did he stop taking them after that?' she whispered, her eyes huge in her pale face.

Adam could tell how much this was hurting her but he was powerless to do anything about it. 'I thought he had until the day he showed up in Theatre, high as a kite. I don't know what he'd taken because I didn't ask him. I just told him to leave and wait for me in my office.'

He ran a hand round the back of his neck, feeling the tension in the knotted muscles. This was even worse than he'd feared it would be and all he could do now was to get it over as quickly as possible.

'As soon as I'd finished in Theatre, I went straight to my office. Keiran was spoiling for a fight and he launched straight in as soon as I went into the room. I won't repeat what he said because he was out of control and had no idea what he was saying. But in the end I had to call Security and have him escorted from the building.'

'That can't be true! Keiran's always been such a…a *gentle* person.'

'He probably is, but drugs can and do change a person's character. Anyway, I knew that I had to report him because his behaviour had gone way beyond what was acceptable, but I wanted him to be aware of what was happening so I went to see him that night.'

'You did? He never told me…'

She broke off and he sighed because there was a lot her brother hadn't told her.

'I went round to his flat and he was a lot calmer than he'd been earlier in the day, far more subdued. I think he'd realised what a mess he'd got himself into because he just sat there and listened to what I had to say.'

'And that was?'

'I told him that I didn't think he was cut out for medicine and that he needed to re-evaluate his life.'

'But can't you see that it was the worst possible thing you could have said to him? All those years of study thrown away because of a silly mistake—'

'A mistake he might not have made if he'd been able to handle the pressure.' He cut her off because he couldn't bear to hear her deluding herself any more. 'Studying medicine is hard and not everyone can handle it. Not everyone can handle the pressure after they've qualified either. Your brother simply couldn't cope and that's why he was behaving the way he was. If he removed some of the pressure, he might just be able to get his life back on track.'

He took a deep breath, wondering if she would believe him, knowing in his heart that probably she wouldn't. 'I did it with the very best of intentions, Kasey. I did it to save your brother's life and I would do exactly the same thing again if the situation arose.'

'To save his life?' she repeated, staring at him.

'Yes. That's what I honestly believed at the time and it's what I still believe today. If your brother had continued along the route he'd chosen, he would have gone on taking drugs and it would have been only a matter of time before he overdosed, or killed a patient. I know you find this is hard to believe, but I did what I thought was right—not just for me or the hospital, but for the patients, and for Keiran himself. I didn't want his death on my conscience. I wanted to help him, and I'm sorry if it didn't work out that way, but I did what I thought was best.'

'I don't know what to say,' she whispered, and he smiled thinly.

'I know. There isn't much anyone can say in a situation like this other than the truth.'

'And that's what you've just told me?'

'Yes.' He met her eyes, wanting her to believe him more than he'd wanted anything else. 'It's the truth, Kasey. I know that and now you have to decide if you believe me.'

He moved away from the window, knowing that he couldn't stand there and watch her tearing herself apart while she tried to decide who to believe, him or her brother.

'I'm just going to fetch something from the Jeep,' he explained, opening the door, even though there was nothing in the car that he needed. 'You have the bedroom. I'll be fine on the couch.'

'If that's what you want…' She trailed off and he heard her take a quick breath before she said quietly, 'Thank you.'

Adam didn't say anything—how could he? He'd just told her things that might have changed her opinion of her brother for ever so what else could he say? How much more pain could he inflict on her?

He left the annexe and walked to the Jeep, got in and closed the door and only then did he allow his emotions to spill over. Resting his head against the steering-wheel, he cried out all the pain and anger that he'd kept stored up for the past five years. But the bitterest tears of all were those he shed for Kasey and the fact that he'd had to hurt her. Nothing he did from this point on in his life would ever feel as bad as this.

CHAPTER EIGHT

'AHA! The prodigals return. So how did it go?'

'Not too badly.'

Kasey summoned a smile when June came hurrying out of the hostel to meet her, hoping that she didn't look as exhausted as she felt. She'd spent a sleepless night, going over and over everything that Adam had told her, so that she'd felt completely drained by the time morning had arrived.

It had been an effort to concentrate as they had dealt with the rest of the children who'd needed to be seen. Fortunately, Adam had refused the offer of lunch after they'd finished by explaining to the nuns that they needed to get back to the hospital. He'd said barely half a dozen words to her on the drive back but she'd not felt much like chatting either. She guessed he was upset because she hadn't said if she believed his story about Keiran, but there was nothing she could do until she was sure in her own mind who was telling her the truth.

She glanced round when she heard the Jeep starting up and bit her lip when she saw Adam drive away without a glance in her direction. The situation seemed to be going from bad to worse and she didn't know how to make things right between them.

'Obviously, you two haven't declared a ceasefire,' June said wryly, leading the way inside. 'Pity. I had high hopes when I heard you were staying away overnight that you'd managed to sort out your differences.'

'The chances of us doing that are less than zilch,' she replied, trying to make a joke of it because it wasn't fair to involve other members of the team. The last thing she wanted was for people to start taking sides. 'We'll need a team of trained negotiators to solve this little problem!'

'Oh, well, you can't win 'em all, can you, love?' June put a kindly arm around her shoulders. 'I've just made a pot of tea so come and have a cup before you do anything else. Do I take it that you're officially off duty now until tomorrow?'

'I suppose so. Adam didn't actually say what he wanted me to do this afternoon,' she explained dryly. He hadn't said much about anything.

'In that case, I'd take it as read that you've got the afternoon off and make the most of it.' June whisked her into the kitchen and sat her down on a chair. 'So what's on the agenda? Lunch at The Ivy followed by a spot of retail therapy at Harvey Nics?'

'I wish!' Kasey laughed out loud. 'More like a good scrub down with carbolic to get all these bugs off me, followed by some laundry. I've been reduced to wearing borrowed knickers so I really think I should get some washing done.'

'Oh, pooh! You can do laundry any time.' June plonked a mug of dark brown tea in front of her then put her hands on her hips. 'You need to live a little, my girl, get out and have some fun.'

'What do you suggest?' she asked, grinning as she sipped the tea because June made it sound as though there were umpteen different options to choose from.

'That we go swimming!' June laughed when she put down the mug and stared at her in surprise.

'Swimming! Are you serious?'

'Yep! Apparently, there's a pool not far from here which the locals use. Matthias told me about it and he said that it should be safe enough for us to go there so long as we don't wander away from the main path. Anyway, a few of us have decided to go for a swim this afternoon so why don't you come with us? It would do you good to have a bit of a break. You look absolutely worn out, if you don't mind me saying so.'

'I am,' Kasey agreed ruefully, because there was no point trying to deny it. 'The only problem is that I've not brought a swimming costume with me.'

'Improvise. Shorts and a bra will do fine,' June said cheerfully. 'That's what I'm going to wear, anyway.'

'Problem solved, then. What time are you leaving?'

June glanced at her watch. 'In about half an hour, if that's OK with you? There's a few folk who are coming as soon as they've finished their shifts.'

'Fine. I'll have just enough time to debug myself first.'

She swallowed the rest of the tea and stood up, grimacing when she spotted the red lump that had formed on the inside of her wrist. 'Something's definitely had a go at me. Look at that.'

'You are taking your antimalaria tablets,' June said worriedly, studying the lump.

'Yes. And I've been wearing long sleeves after dark and dousing myself in mozzie repellent, but that's definitely an insect bite.'

'Then you need to get it checked out,' June said firmly. 'There's no point taking any chances so why don't you have a word with Joan and see what she thinks it is? She's the expert, after all.'

'Good idea. I'll do it when we get back,' Kasey agreed.

She hurried upstairs and showered then changed into shorts and a T-shirt, making sure the bra she chose to wear under it was one that wouldn't go transparent in the water. There was no point drying her hair so she simply tied it back in a ponytail then put on some clean socks and her boots and ran back downstairs. June and Mary were already waiting for her in the hall and a few minutes later the rest of the party started to arrive. They were just about to set off when Adam turned up. He parked the Jeep and came over to them.

'Room for one more?'

'Of course,' June replied cheerfully.

'Give me five minutes and I'll be right with you.'

He hurried into the hostel as June drew her aside. 'Sorry, but I really couldn't refuse to let him come.'

'Of course you couldn't.' Kasey managed to smile but she had to admit that some of the pleasure had suddenly gone out of the day. All she could hope was that Adam would leave her to her own devices, as he'd done all morning.

It was a good fifteen-minute walk to the pool, although it felt much longer because of the heat. However, Kasey had to admit that it had been worth the trek when they got there. The pool was in the middle of a small glade and the water gleamed green and tranquil in the light filtering through the canopy of leaves. Tiny, brightly coloured birds swooped over the water, catching insects, mainly iridescent dragonflies whose wings shimmered in the sunlight. There was even a waterfall at one end of the pool which sent up a cloud of silvery spray. It was the most idyllic place she'd ever seen.

'Wow! It's like something out of one of those adverts you see on the telly,' Mary exclaimed in awe. 'Any minute now some gorgeous, handsome hunk in a loincloth will rise from that water and offer me a chocolate bar.'

'Not if I see him first, he won't!'

Everyone laughed as June stripped off her T-shirt and jumped into the water. Within a few minutes they were all splashing about. Kasey joined in the fun for a while then swam over to the waterfall, ducking beneath the surface so she could come up on the other side. There was a tiny cavern there, its sides covered with huge, curling ferns which grew out of the rock. It was wonderfully cool in there with the curtain of water shielding it from the burning heat of the day and she floated about for a while, enjoying the simple pleasure of doing nothing. She was just thinking that she should go back and join the others when Adam suddenly surfaced beside her, making her gasp in surprise.

He shook the water out of his eyes. 'Sorry. I didn't mean to startle you.'

'It's OK.' She gave him a noncommittal smile then turned to swim back to the waterfall because she knew how quickly the situation could deteriorate when they were on their own.

'By the way, I had a word with Shiloh about the kids at the orphanage and he's agreed to put together another team to fly out here. He's going to see if he can find a couple of counsellors willing to come as well.'

'That's good,' she said, treading water to keep herself afloat.

'Shiloh also told me that he's managed to find another anaesthetist.'

'To replace me?' she said hollowly, her heart sinking.

'Yes. He'll be flying out here on Friday. Apparently, there's another plane-load of supplies being delivered then.'

'So do I take it that I'll be going back to England when the plane returns?' she asked quietly, doing her best not to let him see that she was upset at the thought of leaving.

'Yes.' He sighed wearily. 'It's the best solution, Kasey. You must see that.'

'If you say so.'

She didn't say anything else as she swam back under the waterfall because it would serve no purpose to argue with him. Adam had made up his mind and no amount of protests would make him change it. The rest of the party were still splashing about in the water but she simply couldn't bear to join them so she climbed out and towelled herself dry. She was just putting on her boots when June swam over to her.

'Had enough for one day?'

'Yes. I think I'll go back to the hostel,' she said in a choked little voice. She didn't want to be sent home but there was nothing she could do to stop it happening and especially not after last night. Adam must be keener than ever to get rid of her now and the thought hurt.

'Hey! What's up?' June scrambled out of the water and sat down beside her, looking concerned.

'Nothing. I'm just being stupid.' She took a deep breath as she dabbed her eyes with the hem of her T-shirt. 'Adam just told me that I'll be going home on Friday. It's really silly to get upset because I knew I'd be going back at some point.'

'He isn't still going through with it!' June exclaimed in dismay.

'Apparently.' She summoned a smile. 'Still, look on the bright side. I won't need to keep borrowing knickers from everyone now, will I?'

June laughed but Kasey could tell she was upset by the news. Maybe she shouldn't have told her, although there was no way she could have kept it a secret. Everyone would know soon and the idea of them all knowing that she was being sent home in disgrace was very difficult to deal with but she had no choice.

Again.

She sighed because ever since she'd come to Mwuranda, she'd had little control over what had happened. It was the complete opposite of what she'd hoped for, too. She'd hoped to regain control of her life by facing up to the past but it hadn't turned out that way. It hadn't even helped to hear Adam's side of the story because if she believed his version of events, it meant Keiran had been lying, and it was very difficult to accept that her own brother would have lied to her.

She glanced up when Adam climbed out of the water close to where they were sitting and felt her heart ache when she realised just how much she wanted to believe him. It was just making that final leap of faith that was so difficult, that and the fact that she would then have to face up to what she'd done to him. The thought that she might have hurt him unnecessarily was almost too much to bear.

News of Kasey's imminent departure had spread like wildfire, so that by the time Adam arrived at the canteen for dinner that night, everyone knew she would be leaving on Friday. He tried not to react when he saw more than one hostile look being shot his way, but he wouldn't have been human if he hadn't been upset by the way people were reacting. They'd obviously taken Kasey's side and it wasn't nice to be seen as the bad guy.

He helped himself to a plate of cottage pie and canned vegetables and took it over to a table by the window. Kasey was sitting with June and Mary at the opposite side of the room so he sat down with his back towards them. Picking up his fork, he made himself eat the food but every mouthful tasted like sawdust. When Daniel approached him, he pushed the plate away in relief.

'Look, Adam, I know it isn't my place to say anything but won't you reconsider? Everyone is gutted about Kasey leaving.'

'You're right. It isn't your place to say anything.' He shoved back his chair, glaring at the younger man as he stood up. 'Kasey is going back to England and that's it. My decision is final. Is that clear?'

'Perfectly,' Daniel replied, tight-lipped with anger.

'Good.' Picking up his tray, he carried it back to the

serving hatch and plonked it down on the counter then turned to address everyone in the room. 'If anyone else feels so strongly about Kasey going home, you can always go with her.'

He left the canteen, hearing the buzz of conversation that broke out the minute he'd left. He knew that he'd handled the situation very badly but there was only so much he could stand. He didn't want Kasey to go home any more than anyone else did but it was the only sensible course open to him. He couldn't let her stay and run the risk of making a complete fool of himself by begging her forgiveness. *He* hadn't done anything wrong! It was her brother who'd been at fault...

Although maybe he could have tried harder to find a solution to Keiran's problems, offered him more support, tried to counsel him. At the time he'd believed he'd been doing the right thing but, with hindsight, had he?

His mouth compressed as he let himself out of the front door because he wasn't used to analysing his actions and having all these doubts. He knew there was little hope of him sleeping while he was in this frame of mind so he climbed into the Jeep and drove back to the hospital. Work was the best thing for him at the present time and there was always plenty of that.

David Preston was just crossing the foyer when Adam arrived and he looked at him in surprise. 'How did you know we needed you here? Do you have second sight or something?'

'Must do,' he replied lightly, not wanting to go into the ins and outs of how he happened to be there. 'What's happened?'

'There's been some sort of fracas in town. I'm not sure exactly what happened but we've got three people injured. Two of them have serious stab wounds and the third looks as though he's been badly beaten,' David explained.

'We're going to have to operate on all three so I was just about to send someone to fetch you.'

'We're going to need some more staff as well,' Adam decided. 'There's just Lorraine and Katie on tonight, plus a couple of the local nurses, isn't there? So I'll send someone over to the hostel. Is Tony in the treatment room?'

'Yes. He's trying to stabilise the chap who was beaten up. Looks like he could have a ruptured spleen.'

'That will definitely need sorting out pronto.'

Adam made straight for the treatment room. Tony Bridges was putting a third line into the young man who was lying on the examination couch and he glanced round when Adam appeared.

'I see the cavalry's arrived. That was quick.'

'I was already on my way back here,' he explained briefly, checking the monitor readings. BP was way down and pulse rate wasn't much better—both pointing towards massive internal bleeding and shock. 'The sooner he's in Theatre the better.'

'Amen to that,' Tony declared succinctly, opening the line and squeezing through the fluid. One of the local nurses, Florence, was helping him and Adam drew her aside.

'I need someone to go to the hostel and fetch some of our staff back here. Do you know of anyone who could take a message for me?'

'My son will go, Doctor. He is a good boy and he will be very quick.'

'That would be great. Thanks.'

He found a pad, quickly wrote the message and handed it to her. She hurried away as he turned back to Tony again. 'I'll get everything set up. Bring him through as soon as you're ready.'

'Will do.'

Tony waved a languid hand, his eyes never leaving his

patient as he continued pushing through the fluids. Adam smiled to himself as he made his way out of the building and into the theatre tent. Tony might give the impression of being half-asleep most of the time but he was a first-rate doctor for all that.

He unzipped the outer flap of the tent and let himself in, flicking on the generator as he went so that within seconds the whole place was lit up. The mobile theatre unit was really three tents in one: the first section—the entrance—was the least sterile area so he kicked off his boots and left them there before moving through to the next area which was where they showered and scrubbed up.

Stripping down to his underpants, he grabbed a towel and headed for the showers. He towelled himself dry afterwards and was just fastening the draw cord on a pair of green cotton scrub trousers when someone else came into the tent. Adam paused, the top he'd been about to pull over his head dangling from his hand as he waited for Daniel to join him. He knew that he owed the anaesthetist an apology for the way he'd spoken to him at dinner and there was no time like the present to get it over with. The words were actually forming on his lips when the tent flap lifted and Kasey appeared.

'Where's Daniel?' he demanded, looking past her.

'I asked him to swop with me.'

She let the flap drop back into place and walked over to the bench. Facilities in the mobile unit were, by necessity, communal and he felt a rush of heat in his groin when she turned her back to him and stripped off her T-shirt.

'Was there a particular reason why you wanted to trade places with him tonight?' he ground out, doing his damnedest to prevent the inevitable happening. He failed—miserably—and cursed his treacherous body when he felt it quicken with desire.

'I didn't think it was fair to put him in the firing line

again.' She glanced over her shoulder and he could see the reproach in her eyes. 'Your quarrel is with me, Adam, not Daniel or anyone else on this team. It isn't fair to get at them because they are being supportive of me.'

'It isn't fair to be made to feel like the villain either,' he snapped back, and saw her eyes widen.

'What do you mean?'

'Nothing. Forget it. We have more important things to worry about.' He dragged the top of the scrub suit over his head then jumped when he emerged and discovered that she was standing in front of him.

'I have *never* tried to make out that you are the bad guy.'

'I didn't say you had,' he countered, because he desperately needed to stay focused. All she had on now was a bra and a pair of trousers, and it was far too little for his personal comfort.

'The last thing I want is folk taking sides,' she persisted, seemingly oblivious to his dilemma. 'I would never forgive myself if that happened.'

'Fine.' He swung round but she caught hold of his arm.

'You do believe me, don't you? I know we've had our differences in the past but I would never do or say anything to undermine you in any way, Adam.'

'Yes, I do believe you. Now, if you've quite finished...'

'I don't know why I bother! You won't even try to accept that I genuinely mean what I say.' She spun round on her heel and marched back to the bench.

'I do believe you!' he ground out, his blood pressure reaching danger level as he forced himself to stay where he was and not to go after her. Heat fizzed along his veins as his body made a very positive statement about what might happen if he followed her and he shifted uncomfortably to ease the growing pressure in his loins. 'I do believe you,' he repeated more quietly, but she refused to be mollified.

'You've a funny way of showing it.'

'For pity's sake, Kasey, how do you expect us to have a rational conversation with you in that state!' He swept a hand towards her and saw the colour rush up her cheeks when she realised what he meant.

'Oh!'

'Oh, indeed,' he replied dryly, then chuckled when it struck him how ridiculous the situation was. He shook his head when she looked at him in surprise. 'Crazy, isn't it? I know you hate my guts for what I did to your brother, but I still want you.'

'I don't hate you, Adam.'

'No? Then maybe you should.'

'What do you mean?'

'That perhaps I should have shown more compassion.' He sighed wearily. 'All I can say in my own defence is that I did what I thought was right at the time, and if I got it wrong then I'm sorry.'

'Thank you.' Her voice was choked with tears but she waved him away when he took a step towards her. 'No, please, don't. I shouldn't be getting upset when we have a patient to worry about.'

She quickly made her way into one of the shower stalls and drew the curtain. Adam ran his hands through his hair, wishing he could do something but not sure what. In the end, he followed her example and got ready—scrubbing up and putting on a gown—so that by the time the patient arrived he was fully prepared.

Kasey joined him a few minutes later and set about her job with a precision that hinted that she, too, was making a determined effort not to think about anything apart from her job. Maybe she felt as unsure as he did and he was grateful that she didn't let it show because he didn't think he could have coped with much more that night. It was easier to focus on work than think about all the *what-ifs* that were trying to invade his mind: what if they managed to resolve their differences; what if she decided he wasn't to blame; what if…?

No! They didn't help. They just made him feel more confused. He needed to stick to the facts and not get side-tracked by wishful thinking, and the fact that Kasey had *pretended* to be in love with him was something he couldn't ignore. All the time they'd been together she had been pretending and she'd been very good at it, too, because he'd never once doubted her sincerity and that led him to fact number two.

How could he ever trust her again? If she'd lied to him once, she might do it a second time—and that led him on to fact number three.

He really and truly couldn't face having his heart broken all over again.

'Urine output's dropped.'

Adam glanced up as Kasey updated him on their patient's status. 'He's lost so much blood that kidney failure was almost inevitable. Have we managed to cross-match yet?'

'Joan is still working on it. I'll give him another litre of O-neg for now.'

'And let me know if his urine output drops any further,' he instructed, returning his attention to the task of removing the patient's ruptured spleen. He couldn't count the number of times he'd performed the operation but he also couldn't recall seeing a spleen that had been so badly damaged before. The organ had been literally pulverised and removing it took time, care and patience.

An alarm suddenly sounded on the monitoring equipment and he looked up. Kasey was breaking open a vial of drugs and drawing the contents up into a syringe. She slid the needle into the catheter inserted into the back of the patient's hand, her forehead creasing into a frown as she studied the monitor screen.

'He's asystolic,' she said, moving aside the drapes and reaching for the paddles of the defibrilator. She charged the machine then looked round. 'Clear!'

Adam stepped away from the table as did Lorraine who'd been assisting them. They both waited in silence to see if an output had been established but the monitor showed that the patient still didn't have a heartbeat. Kasey tried twice more to establish a heart rhythm but it was no good. The patient had died from a combination of blood loss and shock, and no amount of hi-tech equipment would bring him back.

'Sorry,' she said, switching off the machines.

'It wasn't your fault,' Adam said bluntly. 'Blame the folk who did this to him because they're the ones who killed him.'

'I guess so.'

Her tone was flat as she began disconnecting all the tubes and leads. Lorraine gave her a commiserating smile as she loaded their instruments onto the trolley and wheeled it away. Kasey smiled back but he could tell that she was genuinely upset. As soon as they were on their own, he moved around the table and stood in front of her.

'There was nothing else you could have done, Kasey. His spleen was in a real mess and heaven knows what other injuries he had as well.'

'I know. It's just hard when you get this far and lose someone, isn't it?'

'It is, but it's also the nature of the job. If people weren't very sick, we wouldn't be trying to help them.'

She gave him a tentative smile. 'You always did have a way of making sense of what happened.'

'Did I? It's nice to know that I have some good points.'

He turned away but she put her hand on his arm and her eyes were troubled when they met his. 'You have a lot of good points, Adam. More good ones than bad, in fact.'

'It doesn't feel that way from where I'm standing,' he said honestly. 'I seem to have done nothing but upset folk recently.'

'And that's all because of me.' She shook her head when he went to speak. 'It's true. I should never have come, should I? I've just ended up making a bad situation worse, and that wasn't what I wanted to do.'

'Why did you decide to come when you knew you'd be working with me?' he asked curiously.

'Stubbornness.' Kasey sighed when he stared at her in surprise. 'I decided that I'd made enough changes to my life because of you and that it was time I stopped running away.'

'Running away? What do you mean by that?'

'I took the job at St Edward's because of you and I left it for the same reason. I didn't want to leave because I enjoyed working there, but obviously I couldn't have stayed after we split up. I found it very difficult to settle into another job after that so I took a series of short-term contracts and moved around a lot.'

She shrugged. 'When I saw the ad for Worlds Together it seemed like the ideal solution. I'd be able to travel abroad and do the kind of work that I'd never done before yet still keep a toehold in the UK through my contract work. I was so geared up to doing it that it was a bolt from the blue when I found out you would be in charge of my first posting.'

'It didn't put you off, though.'

'Oh, yes, it did!' She laughed shortly. 'I almost told Shiloh that I wouldn't be able to go, but then I realised if I did that, you would have won.'

'Won?' His brows rose steeply because he couldn't for the life of him imagine what she meant.

'Yes. My aim was only ever to pay you back for what you'd done to Keiran, but it backfired on me. Big time.'

She stared up at him and he could see the pain that lit her eyes as well as the regret. He knew he really should say something but he couldn't seem to find the right words and she carried on.

'I know I hurt you, Adam, and I'm sorry for that. I just wanted to show you how awful it feels to have your whole life torn apart. I never intended to break your heart and certainly didn't plan on having mine broken as well.'

She smiled sadly when he gasped. 'I can tell that you're shocked but it's true. You see, the one thing I never allowed for was that I would fall in love with you as well.'

'In love with me?'

Adam heard the shock in his voice but it was the very least of his worries. He stared into her face, wondering how it was possible to feel so elated yet so devastated at the same time. Kasey had loved him, *really* loved him, and the thought made him want to turn cartwheels for joy, but that was merely the upside. The downside was all too obvious and it sent him plummeting into the very depths of despair.

She might have loved him in her own way but she'd still put her brother first. *He* could never have done that— he would have put her interests above everything else, moved heaven and earth if it had meant they could stay together. So just how deep could her love have been if she'd been able to walk away and leave him?

'Yes, but don't worry. I don't expect you to believe me.'

She gave him a sad little smile that tugged at his heartstrings. When she turned, Adam gripped her hand.

'I want to believe you, Kasey,' he bit out, his voice trembling with the force of his emotions.

'Do you?' She covered his hand with hers and he felt the tremor that passed through her.

'Yes. It's just…difficult.'

'I know.'

Reaching up, she kissed him softly on the cheek. Adam closed his eyes as myriad feelings washed through him. Joy and happiness, pain and sadness, every kind of emotion from both ends of the spectrum. Turning his head, he captured her lips and kissed her back, gently and with a tenderness that he couldn't have disguised even if he'd wanted to, which he didn't. Maybe it was the wrong thing to do but he was past thinking about the rights and wrongs and was merely reacting.

Kasey's lips clung to his for a second before she drew back, and there were tears in her eyes as she laid her hand against his cheek. 'What we had was very special, Adam, and I shall never regret the time we spent together.'

Adam couldn't speak, he was too choked. And in the end he didn't need to say anything because it appeared that she didn't expect an answer from him.

He took a deep breath as she turned away, held it because if he didn't there would be too much room inside him for all the pain that was waiting to rush in. He knew in his heart that they still hadn't resolved the issues that lay between them but they'd talked, not argued, and that was something positive to hold onto. It was definitely better than believing that Kasey hated him.

CHAPTER NINE

MORNING light filtered through the windows and Kasey woke up, although it was a moment before she realised that she was in the sitting room instead of her bedroom.

She got up and made her way into the hall because falling asleep in odd places had become a habit lately. She'd been too keyed up to sleep when she'd got back to the hostel in the early hours of the morning so had gone into the sitting room while she'd calmed down. Tony Bridges had driven her back from the hospital after Adam had announced that he intended to stay there and would cover for him. Tony had been delighted to get an early finish and hadn't questioned the decision, but she'd understood the reasoning behind it. Adam had needed some time on his own to think about that revelation she'd made.

She went into the kitchen and filled the kettle, taking care not to make too much noise. It was just gone five and everyone else was still asleep. She wasn't on duty until eight that morning and she intended to have her act together by then. She might have made a fool of herself by telling Adam that she'd been in love with him but she didn't intend to run away and hide. She would carry on as though nothing had happened...

If he would let her.

The thought of the repercussions her confession might have was a sobering one. Adam had been shocked when she'd told him that she'd loved him so what if he decided that he couldn't carry on working with her? The thought of not being allowed to work throughout the rest of her stay in Mwuranda was more than she could bear. She

would go mad if she was forced to sit in the hostel, thinking about what had happened! She had to make sure Adam
understood that last night's revelations weren't going to
change anything by never alluding to it again and simply
getting on with her job.

That decided, she made herself a cup of tea and drank
it then went to get changed. June opened a bleary eye as
she crept into the bedroom.

'Have you only just got back?'

'No. I've been back for a while but I fell asleep in the
sitting room,' Kasey whispered, opening a drawer. 'Sorry
about waking you up but I needed some clean clothes.'

'Th's OK,' June mumbled, and promptly went back to
sleep.

Kasey collected what she needed and took a shower. It
was still only five-thirty by the time she'd finished getting
ready, far too early to go back to the hospital, so she went
downstairs and unlocked the front door. There was a faint
mist rising off the trees when she let herself out and the
air smelt wonderfully fresh. It struck her all of a sudden
just how much she was going to miss being there. There
might be many problems in this country but she'd grown
to love it in the short time she'd been there and would like
to return at some point in the future...

Or maybe even sooner because what was to stop her
volunteering to join the new team the agency was putting
together? It wasn't as though there was anything to keep
her in England. Her parents had retired to Portugal a few
years ago and Keiran had gone to live in Ireland, so it
might be just what she needed. She'd been drifting for far
too long and this could be the start of a new phase in her
life, so long as the agency agreed to let her return.

Would they? Or would they refuse to send her back to
Mwuranda because she'd left before her present contract
had run out? It didn't seem fair that her plans might be

scuppered because of the problems she and Adam had been experiencing, so she made up her mind to talk to him about it as soon as she got the chance. If he would agree to vouch for her, there shouldn't be a problem about her securing a place on the new team, but would he do that for her?

She sighed. Each time she came up with a solution, another problem followed it. Nothing was ever cut and dried. Every single thing seemed to hinge on Adam and it wasn't just the effect he'd had on her professional life either. Her personal life had been greatly influenced by him, too. Although she'd been out with several men in the last few years, she'd never met anyone who'd made her feel the way Adam had done. With a sudden flash of insight she realised that it had been the yardstick by which she'd measured every new relationship: she'd compared every man she'd dated to Adam and had found every one of them lacking—and she always would.

Her heart began to race because there was no way she could lie to herself any longer. She was still in love with him and that was why she'd never wanted anyone else. She might have buried her feelings in the past few years but they were still just as strong. It scared her to admit it but what was worse was knowing that he would never feel the same about her. She'd hurt him far too much for him to fall in love with her a second time.

Adam sat on the steps and watched the sun coming up. Sunrise in Africa was always spectacular but he derived very little pleasure that day as he watched the sky turn from shimmering lemon to vibrant orange. He felt completely drained, as though someone had turned on a tap and allowed every drop of energy to pour out of him.

He got up, feeling tiredness dragging at him as he made his way back inside the hospital. His body was desperately trying to tell him that it needed to rest but he refused to listen. He needed to keep busy, needed to fill his mind to stop himself thinking about what Kasey had told him last night…

He groaned when his thoughts immediately whizzed back to that conversation they'd had. Cursing softly, he made his way to the side room where Matthias was sleeping and took the chart off the end of the bed, staring at the notes the night staff had written until the words danced like dervishes before his eyes.

What on earth was he going to do? Should he talk to Kasey about what she'd said or just ignore it?

It all depended on what he hoped to achieve, of course, and he still hadn't made up his mind about that. Did he want Kasey back—with all the risks that might entail—or did he want her out of his life for good so he could restore a modicum of normality to his life? His mind twisted this way and that, and he sighed wearily because it was impossible to know what the answers should be.

'Should I be worried?'

'What?' He swung round when Matthias's voice suddenly interrupted his musings.

'I assume there must be something very wrong if you feel it necessary to study my notes with such concentration,' his friend observed dryly, wincing as he eased himself up against the pillows.

'Oh! No, no. Everything's fine.' Adam quickly replaced the chart, feigning a nonchalance he didn't feel. He desperately wanted to believe that Kasey had been telling him the truth but he was terrified of getting hurt again.

'That is good to know,' Matthias agreed calmly. 'So now that we have established I am not about to meet my Maker in the foreseeable future, why don't you tell me what's really worrying you?'

'Nothing.' Adam strode to the door because he certainly

didn't want to discuss the situation with anyone else. No amount of well-meant advice was going to solve this problem! 'I'll call back later to see you—'

'If you love her then tell her that.'

'I beg your pardon?' He turned and glowered at Matthias.

'You heard me the first time but I'm more than happy to repeat it if it will help you see sense.' Matthias looked him squarely in the eyes. 'If you love Kasey, tell her how you feel.'

'I don't know where you got that idea from.'

'From you. You, my friend, are exhibiting all the classic symptoms.' Matthias held up his hand and began checking off points on his fingers. 'You're short-tempered and constantly on edge. You appear more than a little abstracted at times. You react violently whenever the lovely Dr Harris's name is mentioned…'

'And that's supposed to convince me, is it?' Adam snorted.

'Knowing you, I very much doubt it. You always were too stubborn for your own good, Adam. However, just ask yourself why you are sending her home if you don't have any feelings for her.'

'I already explained why,' he snapped, reaching for the doorhandle.

'I know. And we both know it was a pack of lies.' Matthias looked reproachfully at him. 'I expected better of you, my friend. I thought you had the courage of your convictions, yet you refuse to admit how you feel.'

'You don't know what you're talking about. All right, so at one time Kasey and I did have something going for us, but it's all in the past and I'm certainly not in love with her now!'

'The same as she isn't in love with you?' Matthias smiled. 'I may be confined to this bed but I have eyes in my head and I've seen the way you two behave around one another. There's definitely something there, believe me.'

'I really don't have the time for this,' Adam said abruptly, wrenching open the door. 'The sooner you're back on your feet the better. Maybe it will stop you fantasising about things you know nothing about!'

He left the room, closing his ears to Matthias's mocking laughter. The night staff were getting ready to leave, yawning tiredly as they cleared up in readiness for the changeover. The truck arrived and the day staff climbed out, chattering away as they entered the hospital. It was the start of another day and he should have been pleased that in such a short time they'd managed to get things running so smoothly, but it was difficult to focus on everyday matters when his mind kept switching track.

He made a determined effort as he greeted June, said hello to Joan, then frowned when he spotted Kasey walking up the steps because he'd not expected to see her in work that day. He went to the door, holding up his hand when she murmured good morning and went to slip past him.

'What are you doing here?'

'Coming in to work.'

She tossed back her hair and his hands clenched when he saw pale she looked. It was obvious that she'd been brooding about what had happened and it didn't make him feel any better to know that it had been playing on her mind as well as his.

'There's no need for you to work today,' he said curtly, because he didn't need this kind of pressure. He was having enough trouble sorting out his own emotions without worrying about her! 'You did enough last night so you can take the day off.'

'I did no more than anyone else,' she stated coolly. 'I

don't expect any special favours, Adam, so if you'll excuse me…'

She looked pointedly at the door, leaving him no choice apart from ordering her to leave. The thought of creating a scene was more than he could bear so he stepped aside, promising himself that he would keep things low-key from now until she left. Matthias had sounded so sure of himself but Adam refused to believe that he was still in love with her. Maybe he did still desire her but that was all it was—physical need—and his friend had picked up on it. Love needed trust to survive and that was the one thing he could never do—trust Kasey again.

It was a sobering thought and he tried not to dwell on it as he made a start on the ward rounds. Both of the men who'd been stabbed the previous night were now stable, although they were still heavily sedated. None of the local staff knew who they were so they would have to wait until they regained consciousness before their relatives could be traced. The same applied to the man with the ruptured spleen—they couldn't inform his relatives that he'd died until they knew who he was but, hopefully, they should be able to sort everything out fairly soon.

Adam finished his round and had a quick lunch then went to Theatre and found that he was working with Kasey again. He didn't comment on it as he got ready, determined that he wasn't going to do anything to create a disruption. There were just three days to get through until the plane arrived and took her back to England, and he could hold out that long.

It was a long and particularly gruelling session and Adam was exhausted by the time they finished. He'd been on his feet for almost thirty-six hours and every muscle in his body was demanding a rest. Mary shot him a worried look as they cleared up.

'You need to get yourself to bed. You're absolutely dead on your feet.'

'You're right. I am,' he agreed, because there was no point trying to pretend he was Superman. 'I'm going straight back to the hostel after I've finished up here.'

He swung round only to grind to a halt when he almost cannoned into Kasey who'd been on her way out. 'Sorry,' he said, politely stepping aside.

'My fault,' she countered, and he sighed because they were both behaving like guests at a vicarage tea party. He guessed that she was feeling as wary as he was after last night, but knowing that didn't help very much. Had she told him the truth? Or had it been another pack of lies?

The questions nagged away at him as he followed her into the scrub room. Stripping off his gown, he dumped it into a sack then reached for a towel at the same moment as Kasey went to take it off the shelf.

'Sorry,' he muttered, hastily withdrawing his hand.

'It's OK. You have it.'

'No, you take it. I insist,' he said in exasperation, because all this politeness was starting to get on his nerves.

'Thank you.'

She lifted the towel off the rack and Adam frowned when he spotted the red lump on the inside of her right wrist.

'Is that an insect bite?'

'What…? Oh, yes. I noticed it yesterday and meant to have a word with Joan about it.' She ran her finger over the lump and grimaced. 'I'm not sure if it is a bite, though. It looks more like a boil to me.'

'Let me see.' Adam took hold of her hand so he could examine the lump, sighing when he saw a tiny hole in the centre of the swelling. 'It's not a boil. It looks like you've got something in there.'

'What do you mean?'

'I've seen lumps like this before and they're usually caused by the larvae of various flies. The flies lay their eggs in the seams of clothing that's been left outside to dry and when the eggs hatch, the larvae burrow under the skin.'

'Ugh! Oh, that is so gross. You mean I've got a creepy-crawly living in there?' She stared in revulsion at her wrist and he chuckled.

'It's pretty easy to get rid of it so don't panic. Have your shower then come to the treatment room and I'll sort it out for you.'

He picked up a towel and went into one of the stalls. Kasey was already dressed by the time he finished so they walked back to the hospital together. The treatment room was empty for once so he waved her to the couch.

'Sit down while I find some oil.'

'Oil?' she repeated in surprise as she perched herself on the edge of the couch. 'What do you need oil for?'

'The simplest way to get rid of these little beggars is to cover the swelling with oil. The larva can't breathe so it pokes its head out and you can remove it then with a needle.'

'It's just so disgusting. To think I've been walking round for the past day with that thing in my wrist!'

'It could have been worse. You could have had more than one little freeloader tagging along for the ride,' he consoled her with a grin.

'Thank you very much for those words of comfort,' she retorted as he came back with a small bottle of oil and a sterile needle still in its wrapper.

'You're welcome.' He sat down beside her, placing her arm across his lap while he dribbled a little oil onto the lump.

'What happens now?'

'We wait for it to pop its head out so I can remove it.'

'And I was seriously thinking about volunteering to come back here, too,' she said with a shudder. 'I may need to have a rethink!'

He looked up in surprise. 'What do you mean, come back here?'

'With that new team the agency is getting together. I thought I'd ask if I could be part of it, although I'm not sure if I'll be allowed to return because I'm having to leave before my present contract has ended.'

'Shiloh won't hold that against you. He understands that your return has nothing to do with your ability to do the job.'

'So you would support my request to be part of the new team?'

'I don't know if it's a good idea for you to come back here,' he said slowly, because he hated the thought of her returning to Mwuranda without him. It wasn't that he didn't believe she would make a valuable contribution to the new team—it was the idea of her putting herself in danger again that worried him more.

'Why not?'

'Because it's still very volatile over here,' he said, choosing his words with care. Maybe it was silly to imagine that he could protect her but he didn't know how he would cope with the thought of her being here while he was back in England, although he wasn't sure if it would be wise to tell her that. 'I doubt the situation will settle down for a while yet, so it seems silly to put yourself at risk again.'

'It would be no more risky than this visit has been,' she pointed out reasonably. 'In fact, I'd say it will probably be less dangerous because the locals will have got used to the idea of us working here.'

'I still don't think it's a good idea.'

'Well, I do. There's nothing to keep me in England and

I know I can make a valuable contribution here. It's what I want to do and I just need to know if you will support my request to join the new team.'

'If it's what you want, but you could change your mind when you get home.' He shrugged when she looked sceptical. 'Once you're back in the swing of things, you may have a change of heart. It's not unknown for people to be struck by a burning desire to do good only to have second thoughts when they're back at home.'

'I'm sure it isn't but I know what I want to do.'

'In that case, I'll have a word with Shiloh for you,' he agreed flatly. There was no way he could keep on objecting without explaining why he was so against her returning to Mwuranda. After all, she was a grown woman and free to make up her own mind...

But surely not if it placed her in unnecessary danger?

His heart jolted painfully at the thought of anything happening to her, but there was little he could do to dissuade her if she was determined to return. He couldn't explain his fears to her because it would only lead to more questions, and he could hardly tell her that he didn't want her coming back because he couldn't bear the thought of her getting hurt.

'Oh, look!'

He glanced down and nodded when he saw the head of the larva poking out of the lump. 'Good. I'll get it out with this needle. Just hold still for a moment.'

It only took a few seconds to remove the larva then he cleaned the area and taped a dressing over it. 'That should be fine now but if you have any problems let me know,' he instructed, going over to the sink to wash his hands.

'I will. And I'll check my clothes for any little visitors, too, from now on.'

She shuddered as she got down off the couch and he summoned a smile, hoping she couldn't tell how confused he felt. He'd never imagined he would feel this ambivalent towards her. When he'd found out that she was going to be on the team, his feelings had been very clear, but somewhere along the way they'd changed. He could no longer put his hand on his heart and swear that all he felt was anger. For five long years he'd told himself that he was glad to be rid of her but that was no longer true. How could he want to be rid of her when he loved her so much?

The thought slid into his head before he could stop it and pain shot through him. There was no point denying it any longer. He'd never stopped loving Kasey and that was why he'd behaved the way he had of late. It was little wonder that he'd never formed another relationship since they'd split up; he'd given his heart and all that he was to her and there'd been nothing left for anyone else. He wanted her now, for ever and always, but did he dare tell her that?

Last night she'd said she'd *loved* him but it had been past tense, not present, and he had no idea how she felt about him now. She might still have feelings for him but was it love or something else, like nostalgia, or even pity? He'd already decided that her feelings couldn't have been as deep as his had been and they could easily have changed to some lesser emotion, so was he prepared to take that risk? Could he accept second best if that was all she was able to offer him?

The questions pounded into his head but he was just too tired to deal with them, too tired and too scared because there was no point lying to himself about that either. He was terrified of letting himself hope that she might still love him in case he ended up getting hurt again, so what was he going to do? Say something? Or say nothing?

A rush of black humour bubbled up inside when he realised just how hopeless the situation was. He could be damned if he said anything and damned if he didn't!

CHAPTER TEN

'I JUST came to say goodbye, Amelia. I'm going back to
England tomorrow so I won't see you again. I thought you
might like this little present I brought for you.'

Kasey smiled when the little girl exclaimed in delight
as she handed her a red silk hair scrunchie. It was
Thursday afternoon and she was saying her farewells. The
plane was due to land at Arumba airfield at six a.m. the
following morning and would be leaving again as soon as
the cargo had been unloaded. There wouldn't be enough
time for her to visit the patients tomorrow so she'd decided
to get it over with that afternoon.

She gave Amelia a hug then made her way to Matthias's
room. Sarah was with him and she jumped up when Kasey
went into the room.

'Kasey! How lovely to see you.'

'You, too.' Kasey smiled at the other woman. 'I'm glad
you're here because I was hoping to see you before I left.'

'So it's true that you're leaving?' Sarah said sadly. 'We
were hoping that Adam would change his mind but obviously he hasn't.'

'No.' Kasey shrugged, determined not to let herself get
too emotional because it wouldn't help. 'The plane is due
to leave around eight in the morning so this is my last day
at the hospital. I've really enjoyed working here and hope
that I will be able to come back one day.'

'Adam told me that the agency is going to send out
another team of volunteers,' Matthias agreed. 'There's definitely a need for it and we're very grateful for all the help
we're receiving.'

154

'It's good to know that we've managed to achieve something,' Kasey assured him. 'Did you know that we've had more members of the original staff contact us about returning to work? It looks as though the hospital will soon be back on its feet at this rate. Anyway, I just wanted to say goodbye and say how lovely it's been to meet you.'

She kissed them both, feeling a lump come to her throat when they wished her every happiness for the future. She couldn't imagine ever being happy without Adam. She bit her lip as she made her way to the men's ward because she'd made up her mind not to go down that route but it wasn't easy to stop herself thinking about him all the time. For the past two nights she'd even dreamt about him—dreams that had mixed the past and the present together so that it had been doubly difficult to present a calm front during working hours.

As for Adam, well, he hadn't put a foot wrong. He'd been polite and courteous whenever they'd spoken, thanking her after they'd finished in Theatre, including her in the conversation when they were back at the hostel. He'd been a model team leader and in a way that had made the situation even more stressful because if he'd been upset about her impending departure then surely he wouldn't have behaved with such equanimity?

It was depressing to have to face the truth but there was no point deluding herself. She went into the ward and said goodbye to Florence then popped into the lab and said her farewells to Gordon and Joan who, as usual, were pouring over their microscopes. After that it was time to leave so she went outside and waited for the truck to arrive and ferry everyone back to the hostel. As soon as she got back, she went up to the bedroom and packed. June came in as she was zipping up her bag.

'So it looks like you really are leaving us, then?'

''Fraid so.' Kasey put the bag by the door and smiled

at her. 'Thanks for everything, June. You've been a real friend and helped me find my feet. I really appreciate it.'

'Oh, get away with you! I haven't done anything. If you've fitted in, it's because everyone likes you and appreciates how hard you work.'

Kasey felt a lump come to her throat and turned away before she made a fool of herself by crying. 'Well, whatever, it's been great working with you. I'm going to miss you all such a lot.'

'We're going to miss you, too. I only wish…' June broke off and sighed. 'There's no point going over it all again, is there? I'll see you downstairs.'

'I won't be long.' She summoned a smile although she knew what June had been going to say before she'd thought better of it. She, too, wished that Adam would change his mind but it wasn't going to happen. 'I intend to make my last night in Mwuranda one to remember so how about we hold a party? There's an old stereo system in the storeroom so maybe we could get that out and play some music.'

'Brilliant idea! Leave it to me. I'll get it all sorted out.'

'Thanks.'

Kasey sat down on the bed after June hurried away, needing a few moments on her own before she joined the party. She glanced round when someone tapped on the door and felt her pulse quicken when she saw Adam standing outside. He'd obviously just got back from the hospital and she couldn't help noticing how drawn he looked. The past few days had taken their toll on him, too, and all of a sudden she wished that she could make things right between them. The thought of him still thinking badly of her after she'd returned to England was more than she could bear.

'I thought I'd see if you needed a hand,' he explained, coming into the room.

'No. It's fine, thanks.' She pointed to her haversack. 'I'm all packed and ready to leave in the morning.'

'Oh, right. Fine.' He turned to go but she knew that if she didn't take her chance now there might not be another one.

'I'm really sorry, Adam, about everything.'

'And I'm sorry, too, Kasey.' He turned to face her and she saw the pain in his eyes. 'I haven't handled this situation very well…'

'You did your best.' She couldn't bear to hear him apologise when it wasn't his fault. 'It was bound to be difficult, having me on the team.'

'But I should have been able to get over that. I don't normally have a problem separating my personal life from my professional one, but there again I've never been in this situation before.'

'I'm sure you haven't. But I'd like to think that we can part as friends instead of enemies.'

'I certainly don't think of you as my enemy, Kasey,' he said, his deep voice throbbing in a way that made heat suddenly pool in the pit of her stomach.

Kasey rose unsteadily to her feet. It had sounded as though he'd really meant that but was she reading too much into it? 'Neither do I. I just wish…' She broke off, unsure how much to say, and he frowned.

'You wish what?'

'That you would forgive me for what I did. But I know it's too much to expect. I played a really rotten trick on you, Adam, and I'm sorry.'

'I have forgiven you,' he said, half under his breath, and she looked at him in surprise.

'You have?'

'Yes. How about you? Have you forgiven me for what I did to your brother?'

Kasey paused, searching her heart, feeling the relief that

welled inside her all of a sudden. 'Yes! I realise now that you never deliberately set out to hurt Keiran.'

'Do you? You're sure about that?' he asked with an urgency that surprised her.

'Yes. Oh, I don't know why Keiran led me to believe that you were to blame. Maybe he found it too difficult to admit that it was his own fault his life had fallen apart, but I do know that you didn't set out to hurt him. You did what you thought was right for everyone concerned and that's what matters most.'

'I can't tell you how glad I am to hear you say that.' He crossed the room and there was a new intensity in his gaze as he stared into her eyes. 'It's been unbearable to know that you thought I would be so cruel.'

'It must have been hard for you,' she said, biting her lip because there was no way she could doubt that he was telling her the truth. Her accusations had hurt him and it made her feel terrible to know that she'd piled pain on top of pain.

'It was, but we have to move on, put what happened behind us. Maybe we can…'

He trailed off when Katie suddenly appeared. Kasey saw his face close up and it was all she could do to hide her frustration in front of the other woman.

'Oops! I hope I'm not interrupting anything,' the young nurse exclaimed.

Adam shook his head. 'Of course not. I was just checking to see if Kasey needed a hand but she's got everything covered. I'll see you both at dinner.'

With that he was gone, striding along the corridor before Kasey could stop him. She took a deep breath and did her best to respond as Katie chattered happily on about the impromptu party that was being organized, but she couldn't help wondering what would have happened if they hadn't been interrupted. Adam had had something on his mind and it was frustrating to feel as though she'd come so close to making a breakthrough...

She sighed because she was probably deluding herself if she imagined he'd been about to declare his love for her! The likelihood of that happening was non-existent. If he'd cared about her, he certainly wouldn't be sending her home in the morning.

June had pulled out all the stops and the party was a huge success. Everyone seemed to be enjoying themselves apart from him.

Adam sat on the sidelines and watched as everyone danced to the old-fashioned records they'd found packed away in the storeroom. June and Gordon danced past with more verve than skill and he smiled at them but it was an effort to appear upbeat when he was literally counting the minutes until Kasey left.

He'd come so close to blurting out that he still loved her. If they hadn't been interrupted, he would have done it but it would have been a mistake. Maybe he didn't know how he was going to let Kasey go but, equally, he didn't know if he should ask her to stay. Was he *really* prepared to take such a risk with his heart for a second time?

He stood up abruptly, intending to make his escape while everyone was occupied, but just then Kasey came over to him. Like the other women in the group, she'd made an effort to dress up for the party and he couldn't help thinking how gorgeous she looked. It made no difference that she was wearing the same clothes she'd worn throughout her stay in Mwuranda—cotton trousers and a long-sleeved shirt—because she still looked stunningly beautiful to his eyes. It was hard to behave calmly when he longed to sweep her into his arms and tell her how much he loved her, but he didn't have a choice. He was too much of an emotional coward to declare his feelings.

'Would you like to dance, Adam?' she asked, smiling up at him.

He opened his mouth to explain that he'd been about to go to bed but for some reason the words didn't come out the way he'd planned they should. 'Thank you. I'd love to.'

'Good.'

She treated him to another dazzling smile as she led the way to the centre of the room. Daniel was changing the record and they waited until an old-fashioned waltz started to play. Adam held out his arms and she stepped into them, fitting herself lightly against him as they began to dance to the lilting strains of the music, and it was like nothing he'd experienced before.

He'd never been a particularly good dancer, although he could find his way around a dance floor when pushed, but this was different. Every step they took matched seamlessly, every turn was perfectly in harmony. By the time the record ended, everyone else had stopped to watch them and he laughed when a spontaneous burst of applause broke out as the last chords faded away.

'Thank you kindly,' he said, bowing to their audience. He swept Kasey in front of him, grinning when she curtseyed in best theatrical fashion. 'We shall now retire so that you don't feel overawed by having to compete with us.'

A series of boos and catcalls greeted this suggestion and Kasey chuckled as he led her off the floor. 'They'll be throwing ripe tomatoes at us if you aren't careful!'

'Not if we beat a hasty retreat. I don't know about you but all that dancing has worn me out. How about we take a breather?'

'Fine by me.'

She followed him out of the sitting room, pausing when

Adam stopped and glanced at the front door. 'Fancy a stroll?'

'So long as you promise we won't get shot at this time.' She grinned when he frowned. 'I'm only kidding. It should be safe enough so long as we stay close to the building, shouldn't it?'

He nodded as he led the way outside and took a long look around. 'Should be, although there's no guarantee, of course.'

'I'll risk it if you will.'

She walked down the steps, turning right when she reached the bottom, and he followed her. There was a full moon that night and he heard her sigh as she paused to look up at the sky.

'It's so beautiful here. Just look at that sky! You can't see the stars so clearly at home because of the light pollution. But this is just amazing.'

'It is,' he said huskily, his eyes focused on her rather than on the heavens. She looked so beautiful as she stood there in the moonlight that he couldn't resist touching her. Raising his hand, he let his fingers trace the gentle curve of her cheek and felt her flinch.

'Please, don't do that, Adam,' she whispered. 'I don't think I can bear it.'

'And I don't think I can bear not to touch you,' he said just as softly and with a catch in his voice.

She turned to face him and he saw the tears that shimmered in her eyes. 'I wish we could go back to the beginning and start all over again.'

'So do I but it isn't possible.' He cupped her cheek, feeling the dampness of her tears on his fingers. 'We can only go forward from this point on, do what we think is right for both of us.'

'And what is the right thing to do?' She covered his hand with hers, pressing it against her face so that he could feel the warmth of her skin flowing into him like a living force. 'Is it right that I should go back to England when I want to stay here? Because I do, Adam. I really do!'

'I don't know if sending you home is the right thing to do but it's the only way I can deal with this situation,' he said honestly. 'Having you here just makes me feel more mixed up. I don't know if I'm on my head or my heels most of the time and I can't live like this, Kasey.'

'But how do you know it will get better if I go back to England?'

'I don't. And that scares me, too, because I'm not someone who copes well with uncertainties. It's the way I'm made. I know I can come across as cold and unyielding but it was how I was brought up. My parents discouraged any shows of emotions so I find it difficult to deal with my feelings.'

'And what I did to you didn't help,' she said, her voice catching.

'No, it didn't. I suppose I retreated into myself even more. That's probably why I've been so evil-tempered of late,' he explained, aiming for levity and falling far short of the mark.

'The situation would have tried the patience of a saint so I don't blame you for that.'

'Thank you.' He let his hand fall to his side because it was too tempting to keep it there, too tempting to let it stray but that wouldn't be fair. Making love to her the night before he sent her away was the last thing he should be thinking about if he hoped to live with himself in the future.

He took a deep breath and used it to damp down his ardour. 'I'm afraid, Kasey. That's the truth of the matter. I'm scared that I might get hurt again and it's easier to send you home than risk that happening.'

'I would never hurt you again, Adam,' she said fervently. 'I—'

'No.'

He laid his fingers against her lips because he couldn't bear to hear her say that she loved him in case it wasn't true. Oh, she might genuinely believe that she still had feelings for him, but they'd been through a lot in the last two weeks and her emotions were bound to be in turmoil. He didn't think he could stand it if he let himself hope that she really loved him, only to have his dreams shattered when she realised that she'd made a mistake.

'The past couple of weeks have been an emotional time for both of us so let's not say anything we might regret. Let's just be glad that we can part as friends.'

'If that's what you want…?'

'It is.' He drew her to him, held her against him while he savoured this last, too-brief moment then let her go. 'Thank you for everything you've done while you've been here, Kasey. I'm going back to the hospital now so I won't be here in the morning when you leave. Have a safe journey.'

'And that's it? You're sure you want me to leave like this?'

'Yes. I'm sure.'

He turned away and it was the hardest thing he'd ever had to do, to walk away and leave her standing there. Climbing into the Jeep, he started the engine, not allowing himself to look back as he drove away because he couldn't bear to see her standing there, where he'd left her.

Tears clouded his vision and he blinked hard as he turned onto the road. He had done the right thing—the only thing—but it didn't feel like that. It felt as though he'd ripped out his own heart and thrown it away, thrown away any chance he might have had of happiness in the future. There was only one Kasey Harris, only one woman he would ever love, and he had just sent her away!

'Now, make sure you phone me, won't you? Here's my number, and here's my address as well in case of any problems.'

'Thank you.'

Kasey tried to smile but the tears that had been threatening ever since she'd got up that morning suddenly spilled over. It was just gone five and she was about to set off for the airfield. June had insisted on getting up to see her off, although, thankfully, the rest of the team were still in bed. She heard June sigh as she gave her a hug.

'I wish Adam was here so I could knock some sense into him. He must be out of his mind to let you leave like this!'

'He said his goodbyes last night,' Kasey told her, fishing a tissue out of her pocket and drying her eyes.

'Did he now? Well, he should have had the sense to see what a mess he was making, shouldn't he?' June glowered. 'For an intelligent man, he can be very dim at times, that's all I can say.'

'You mustn't blame him, June. He only did what he thought was right. For him and for me,' she added, because she didn't want Adam taking the blame for this when it wasn't his fault.

'And the right thing to do is to send you home when you want to stay?' June shook her head. 'Sounds crazy to me, but who am I to comment? Anyway, have a safe journey and make sure you phone me when I get back so we can catch up on all the gossip.'

'I will. Promise.'

Kasey gave her a hug then got into the truck. Lester was driving her to the airfield and he was obviously keen to be on his way because he set off as soon as she'd slammed

the door. She clung to the seat as they raced through the
town. They bypassed the hospital and she quickly averted
her eyes because she didn't think she could bear it if she
happened to see Adam as they passed the building. Last
night had shown her how stupid it would be to hold out
any hope that he might admit that he loved her. Now she
had to concentrate on the future and start rebuilding her
life. It wasn't going to be easy but she would contact
Shiloh when she got back and tell him that she was inter-
ested in returning to Mwuranda. If she filled every waking
moment with work then she might just survive.

The plane had already landed by the time they got to
the airfield. Kasey got out of the truck and went to find
her replacement, a man in his fifties called Ian Alexander.
She introduced him to Lester then waved them off on their
way back to the hospital. It was all over and done with in
a couple of minutes and she felt a little deflated about how
easy the switch had been made. Come tomorrow, she
would be just a memory as the team got used to working
with their new anaesthetist.

The crew were supervising the cargo being unloaded so
she went to speak to them rather than dwell on that
thought. They were obviously busy so she merely in-
formed them she was there. Several trucks were lined up
near the cargo doors so she sat on her haversack and
watched as the goods were loaded onto them and ferried
away. She was still sitting there when there was a burst of
gunfire and all hell broke out as the soldiers, who were
guarding the airfield, started racing across the tarmac.

Kasey jumped to her feet and ran towards the plane,
seeking cover, but one of the crew intercepted her.

'Don't go in there. If they start firing at the plane it
could explode,' he shouted, pointing towards a tanker that
was in the process of refuelling the aircraft.

'What should we do?'

'Get as far away from the plane as possible. And keep your head down!'

He raced away, heading towards the run-down terminal building, and she ran after him. Bullets were whining overhead and she ducked when one whizzed past her ear then gasped when she saw the man in front of her suddenly fall to the ground. He was clutching his leg so she knew he must have been hit, but there were shots coming from all directions now.

Dropping to the ground, Kasey crawled towards him. His leg was bleeding heavily and she could see a shard of bone sticking out of the flesh. Taking off her shirt, she managed to tie it around his leg as a makeshift pressure bandage but he was in a bad way.

'We have to get you inside so I can look at your leg,' she shouted over the roar of gunfire. 'Can you crawl to the terminal? It's the only bit of cover around here, I'm afraid.'

'I'll try.'

The man's face contorted with pain as he began to inch his way across the stony ground. He made slow progress and Kasey shot a desperate look behind her, hoping that someone would come and help them, but everyone else had taken cover now. All she could see—and hear—were the soldiers responding to the enemy's fire.

It was the most scary ten minutes of her entire life and she was drenched with sweat by the time they crawled inside the empty building. She kicked the door shut behind them and helped the crewman crawl behind the reception desk. It would be safer there if anyone started shooting at the building. Her shirt was already soaked through with blood so she stripped it off his leg then helped him out of his T-shirt so she could use it to staunch the bleeding.

'I want you to stay as still as possible,' she instructed, wadding the T-shirt into a ball and placing it over the wound in his leg. Taking off her belt, she used it to bind the pad in place, being careful not to put any pressure on the broken ends of bone.

She wiped her bloody hands down her jeans and nodded. 'That should help to control the blood loss if you don't move about too much.'

'I don't feel much in the mood for dancing,' he said wryly, and she laughed.

'I'm sure you don't. I'm Kasey Harris, by the way. I'm a doctor.'

'At least I found the right person to get holed up with.' He held out his hand and grinned at her. 'Andy Burton. I am—or rather I was—the navigator.'

'Nice to meet you, Andy, although the circumstances could have been better.' Kasey shook hands then checked his leg. The pressure pad seemed to be working because there was a lot less blood flowing from it.

'That's not looking too bad now so just stay there while I see if I can find you something to drink. We need to keep your fluid levels up.'

'OK, but be careful. Keep well away from the windows.'

'Will do.'

Kasey crawled out from behind the counter and cautiously stood up. There wasn't much left inside the building but she could see an old vending machine in the corner which looked as though it still contained some cans of lemonade. Bending double, she made her way towards it, taking care that she wasn't seen as she passed in front of the windows. The battle was still raging outside but, thankfully, the action seemed to be confined to the area surrounding the plane now. With a bit of luck the soldiers would be able to hold off the rebels until reinforcements arrived.

The vending machine did, indeed, contain some cans of drink. The only problem was getting at them. Kasey tried thumping the machine a couple of times but it didn't achieve very much. In the end she had to resort to smashing the glass panel in the front which she did with the aid of an old plant pot which she found in the corner.

'I like your style.' Andy grinned when she returned with a couple of cans of cola tucked into each pocket. 'Why be boring and put money in the slot if you can smash your way in?'

'So long as you can vouch that it was necessary,' she retorted. 'It won't do a lot for my reputation if I get charged with stealing!'

She popped the tab on one of the cans and handed it to him then checked his leg again, paying particular attention to the pulse in his ankle because she wanted to be sure the artery hadn't been compromised. Fortunately, she could feel a fairly strong pulse there so that was one less thing to worry about, although continued blood loss was going to be a problem. Although the bleeding had slowed, it hadn't stopped completely and her main concern was the length of time they would be holed up in the terminal building.

She popped the top off another can of cola and allowed herself a small sip of the tepid liquid before she placed the can safely on a shelf. Andy might need it more than she did although, hopefully, they would be rescued before it became an issue. News of the attack must have spread by now and the army would send reinforcements so they just needed to be patient and wait for help to arrive.

Just for a moment she wondered what would happen if nobody came to help them. The rebel fighters had a reputation for being ruthless and she couldn't imagine they would spare much thought for her and Andy. All of a sudden she found herself wishing that she'd told Adam that she loved him when she'd had the chance. Maybe he hadn't wanted to hear it last night but she would have felt so much better knowing that she'd told him the truth. Now she was overwhelmed with regret that she might never get the chance to tell him how she felt.

Adam was in Theatre when he heard about the attack on the airfield. June had popped back to the hospital to fetch some more dressings and she came rushing back with the news.

'When did it happen?' he demanded.

'About an hour ago,' June explained, glancing worriedly at the clock.

'So the plane hadn't taken off when the rebels attacked,' he bit out.

'No. It was still being unloaded. They think the rebel forces were after the cargo.'

June bit her lip and Adam could see the same fear in her eyes that must be in his. They both knew that the rebel fighters would stop at nothing to get at the cargo and the thought of Kasey being caught in the crossfire was too much to bear. It was only the fact that he couldn't afford to let his emotions get the better of him when he was in the middle of an operation that kept him focused.

He turned to Daniel and began to rap out orders. 'I want to get this sorted out a.s.a.p. so let's make sure that nothing holds us up.'

Daniel nodded as Adam bent over the table and carried on with a steely determination, refusing to allow himself to imagine what might be happening at the airfield. He wouldn't be able to function if he thought about the danger Kasey was in. It took fifteen minutes before he was able to sew up and they were the longest fifteen minutes of his life.

He dragged off his mask and headed for the exit and nobody tried to stop him. His gloves went into the waste sack, his gown into the hamper then he was outside. The

Jeep was parked in front of the hospital so he got in and started the engine, gripping the steering-wheel as all the images he'd kept at bay suddenly crowded into his head: Kasey cowering beneath a hail of bullets; lying injured and bleeding; maybe…

'No!'

He wasn't aware that he'd shouted the word out loud because he was no longer functioning on a rational level. All he could think about was getting to Kasey before something terrible happened to her. *He'd* sent her to the airfield that day and *he'd* put her in danger. He wouldn't want to carry on living if anything happened to her because there would be no point. If Kasey died, his life may as well be over.

Afterwards, he remembered nothing of the drive to the airfield: one minute he'd set off and the next he was there. There was a road block around the perimeter gates, with armed soldiers manning the barrier, but he drove straight through it, hearing the ricochet of bullets bouncing off the back of the Jeep as they fired at him. He could see the plane sitting on the apron and hear gunfire echoing across the airfield but it seemed to be happening at a distance. He couldn't see Kasey and that was the only thing that mattered—finding her and making sure she was alive.

An armed vehicle suddenly appeared on his right and he had to swerve to avoid it, but it kept on coming, forcing him towards the fence so that he had to stop. Adam jumped out and strode over to it, ignoring the gun that was pointed straight at his chest.

'I'm a doctor from the hospital. One of my staff is here and I want to know where she is.'

The soldier looked uncertainly at him, unsure what to do in the face of authority. 'There is a woman and a man in the terminal,' he said at last.

He pointed towards a run-down building near the edge

of the runway but Adam was already racing back to the Jeep. He put his foot flat on the accelerator and raced across the airfield, swerving to a halt outside the terminal building. He could hear shots being fired but he didn't know if they were being fired at him and didn't care. Kasey was inside and he had to be with her!

He shouldered the door open and there she was, sitting on the floor behind the counter, her clothes covered in blood. She gasped when he appeared and he heard her say his name but he didn't wait to hear anything else.

Dropping to his knees, he hauled her into his arms and kissed her—kissed her with every scrap of pent-up fear, kissed her with every scrap of love, and the next moment she was kissing him back and everything that had been so terribly wrong a moment before was suddenly all right.

'I love you,' he ground out when he raised his head, and she laughed shakily.

'You chose one heck of a moment to tell me that!'

'I can't think of a better one, can you?'

'No, I can't,' she whispered, touching his cheek as though she needed the contact more than anything else.

Adam turned his head so he could press his lips into her palm, wondering if there would ever be a more glorious moment than this. 'I love you,' he repeated, softly and with such sincerity that his own eyes filled with tears as well as hers.

'And I love you, too,' she said, smiling at him even though there were tears streaming down her face.

All of a sudden they were clinging to each other, holding on tight because they both knew how close they'd come to losing one another. It was another wonderful moment, and he had no idea what would have happened if they hadn't been interrupted.

'I hate to break up this very touching reunion, folks, but

I think the shooting may have stopped. How about we get out of here so you can continue this in private?'

Adam glanced at the man lying beside Kasey and chuckled. 'I don't know who you are but I can tell we're going to be friends because we're on the same wave length!'

He stood up, holding out his hand to help Kasey to her feet. 'I've got the Jeep outside. Stay there while I check what's happening.'

'Be careful, Adam,' she said, clinging to his hand.

'I will.'

He kissed the tip of her nose then took a deep breath before he cautiously opened the door and even more cautiously peered out. He didn't need the warning because he had no intention of taking any more risks that day. He had too much to look forward to now to take any more chances!

CHAPTER ELEVEN

'WHERE is everybody?'

'Out.'

Kasey grinned when she saw the surprise on Adam's face. It was midday and they'd just got back to the hostel after operating on Andy Burton's leg. Despite the extensive blood loss, it had gone extremely well and Andy was now comfortably ensconced in the main ward. She wasn't sure what he had told the others but obviously some mention had been made about her and Adam's reunion because June had been grinning like a Cheshire cat when she'd waved them off. Now Kasey chuckled as she slipped her arm into Adam's and snuggled against him.

'I think our patient might have said something so everyone is trying to be tactful by giving us some time on our own.'

'Oh, I see. Nice chap, that, has a sound grasp of what's important, hasn't he?' He swung her round to face him and kissed her on the mouth, sighing when she immediately responded. 'Mmm, that feels so good. It's the sort of medicine that cures a lot of ailments.'

'Sore toes as well as broken hearts,' she suggested, laughing up at him.

'Probably, although I can only vouch for the latter at the moment.' He kissed her again then led her over to the couch and sat down, pulling her onto his knees. 'Have I told you that I love you, Kasey Harris?'

'You may have mentioned it but you can always refresh my memory if you're so inclined.'

'Oh, I'm very much inclined,' he growled, kissing her with a hunger that soon had her clinging to him.

'We really need to do something about that,' she said dreamily a short time later. 'Inclinations as strong as those need attending to poste-haste.'

'And they will be attended to if I have my way but first I want to clear up a few things.'

'Uh-oh! I'm not sure I like the sound of that.' She drew back and looked at him. 'Actions seem to work best for us, Adam, so why don't we stick to that for now?'

'Because I don't want anything to spoil what we have. It's too precious to take any risks with. *You* are too precious, my love.'

'Oh, darling!' She kissed him on the mouth, wishing there was some way she could make up for all the pain she'd caused him. 'I'm so sorry about what I did to you. I know I told you that last night but it needs repeating. I never expected it to have such devastating consequences for either of us.'

'It was devastating,' he said truthfully. 'I loved you so much and when you told me that you'd deliberately led me on and why it was like a kick in the teeth. That's why I said all those awful things to you at the time, and I'm so sorry about that—'

'Don't! I deserved everything I got. I hurt you and it wasn't fair because you never set out to ruin Keiran's life.'

'So you do really believe that? In your head as well as your heart, I mean?'

'Yes.'

She heard the anxiety in his voice and knew how important her answer was to him, but he needn't have worried because she no longer had any doubts. What had happened that day had simply reinforced her view that Adam would never have behaved so cruelly towards her brother.

'I'm absolutely sure. It just isn't in your nature to behave so callously. What you said to Keiran was said with the best of intentions and when I next speak to him, I shall make sure we clear up the situation once and for all.'

'I don't want you falling out with him because of me,' he said in concern. 'I know how much Keiran means to you.'

'He does. He's my brother and I love him very much, but he needs to face the truth just as I did.'

'Maybe he didn't intentionally mislead you.'

'What do you mean?'

'That Keiran wasn't really himself at the time.' He sighed. 'He probably did things which would be alien to him normally.'

'You're right. You already told me how he behaved when you confronted him and it was totally out of character. The drugs were affecting him far more than he realised,' she said sadly.

'Maybe he was ashamed, too, because he knew that what he was doing was wrong. That's probably why he couldn't face telling you the truth and found it easier to blame someone else. In a way, I can understand how he felt because his whole life was in such a mess by that stage.'

'You're too generous,' she said softly, bending to kiss him.

'It's easy to be generous when you have so much to look forward to. Your brother has been through a rough period in his life and all we can do is hope that he sorts himself out.'

'He is trying to get back on track, but I still think he needs to face up to what he did.'

'Then maybe you should talk to him when we get home and get everything settled, once and for all.' He smiled at her. 'I'd feel much happier if I knew this was never going to become an issue between us again in the future.'

'It won't, but if it means that much to you then I'll go and see Keiran as soon as we get back.'

'Good.' He kissed her again then sighed in bemusement. 'And to think I was too scared to admit how I felt about you, too. I can't believe I was such a coward!'

'A coward who came galloping to my rescue in his trusty Jeep,' she teased, and he laughed.

'Hmm, there's different sorts of cowardice—although I'm hoping not to have to repeat today's little episode, thank you very much. Dodging bullets is not my idea of a fun day out but there was no way I was leaving you there in danger.'

'My hero!' She pretended to swoon, then gasped when he extracted his own particular brand of punishment. The kiss was long and increasingly hungry so that she was clinging to him by the time it ended.

'Seeing as we have the place to ourselves, how would you feel about us making the most of the opportunity?' she asked, smiling at him. 'I mean, everyone's gone to a great deal of trouble to make sure we aren't interrupted, so it seems rude not to show our appreciation.'

'Good point. So what do you suggest?'

'That we have a nice cool shower…then a nap.'

'A nap?'

'Yes. After all the excitement we've had today we really need to rest,' she told him, her tongue very firmly in her cheek.

'You can rest if you like but I have other ideas!'

He swept her into his arms and carried her towards the stairs. Kasey giggled as she clung to him.

'Careful! You don't want to do yourself a mischief. It won't look good if the others get back and find you laid up in bed with a pulled muscle, will it?'

'I couldn't give a damn so long as you're in the bed with me,' he said firmly, carrying her up the stairs. Kicking open the bathroom door, he let her slide to her feet and smiled wolfishly at her. 'Were you thinking of showering on your own or sharing?'

'Sharing sounds good to me so long as there's enough room for two in that tiny little stall.'

'I'm sure we can both fit in…if we stand very close together,' he assured her, his deep voice throbbing in a way that made an answering pulse beat in the pit of her stomach.

He bent and kissed her softly on the mouth then started to unbutton her blouse, interspersing each button being opened with another kiss so that she was breathing hard by the time the last one had been undone. He slid the blouse off her shoulders then bent and kissed her throat, letting his mouth slide down until his lips were nuzzling the top edge of her white cotton bra. He drew back and smiled at her.

'You next.'

Kasey's hands were trembling as she began to work the tiny buttons down the front of his shirt out of their buttonholes but they soon steadied because it was such an enjoyable experience. Little by little a bit more of Adam's muscular chest was appearing as the cotton parted, and it was the best incentive in the world to get the job done. The final button popped out and she spread the shirt wide open while she placed a kiss on his breastbone, the tip of her tongue snaking out so that she could taste the slightly salty flavour of his skin. He groaned deeply.

'Now you're taking advantage.'

'I am. Are you objecting?'

'No way! Not so long as I can take advantage of you.'

His hands had slid behind her while he was speaking and the next second she felt the catch on her bra being unhooked. All that was holding it in place were the straps and Adam soon dispensed with them—sliding them off her shoulders and down her arms. Her nipples were already peaking before he touched her and she closed her eyes when she felt a wash of sensation rush through her whole body as he caressed her, cupping her breasts in his palms and stroking her nipples with his thumbs.

'Adam,' she murmured, as the need inside her began to build.

'I know,' he said huskily. 'I know!'

He pulled her to him and held her tightly against him as the waves of pleasure grew inside them both then gently set her away from him and unfastened the snap on the waistband of her jeans. His hands were gentle, reverent, as he eased them over her hips and down her thighs. Kasey stepped out of them and kicked them aside then it was her turn so she unbuckled his belt and drew it through the loops, tossed it aside then unsnapped the fastener and drew down the zip.

Adam caught hold of her hand and pressed it against him and she shuddered when she felt the hardness of his erection. He wanted her as much as she wanted him and the proof of his desire for her was like balm to her soul because she'd never thought he would feel like this a second time.

'I never thought you could love me again,' she said, her voice catching.

'I never thought I would either, but I couldn't help myself.'

He kissed her hungrily and held her to him so she felt the tremor that passed through his strong body, and she loved him all the more because he was letting her see that he was vulnerable, too. Reaching up, she kissed him on the lips, telling him with her mouth how much he meant to her, before she pulled away and slipped out of her panties then turned on shower and stepped beneath the spray.

Adam got in beside her, holding her to him as the water

flowed over their heads and down their bodies, cooling their skin but making the heat inside them seem all the hotter because of that. When he picked up the bar of soap and ran it over her breasts and stomach she shuddered. He handed her the soap and stood patiently as she lathered his skin, her fingers working the scented bubbles into the dark hair on his chest before she frowned when she felt the puckering of old scar tissue. Wiping the lather away, she stared at the injury.

'What *is* that?'

'I was shot when I was over here the first time.' He shrugged when she gasped in dismay. 'It healed really well and has never caused me a problem.'

'That's not the point. June told me that you'd stayed on after the civil war broke out but I didn't realise you'd been shot. Why on earth did you put yourself at risk that way?'

'Because it didn't seem to matter all that much what happened to me.'

Her eyes filled with tears. 'Because of me?'

'Yes. But that's all in the past now so let's not spoil things by dwelling on the mistakes we both made.'

He dropped a kiss on her lips then looked pointedly at the bar of soap. She laughed softly as she soaped her hands and ran them over his broad chest again then let them move lower until he suddenly pulled away, a wry smile curving his beautiful mouth.

'That had better be off limits for now if we hope to get beyond the shower stage.'

'Oh!'

Heat flooded through her when she realised what he meant and he laughed softly and so sexily that she ignored the danger and carried on.

'I did warn you,' he gritted out as he pulled her to him.

'You did but I don't care if we don't make it to the bedroom!'

'Good.'

Their coupling was swift and passionate as the water pounded down on them, each thrust seeming more potent because their skin was slick with water and so sensitive because of that. Their love-making had always been a success but there was a new intensity about it now, a hunger that sprang from the fact that they'd had such a long abstinence. When it was over, Adam rested his forehead against hers and she could feel him trembling.

'I have never wanted anyone the way I want you, Kasey. And I never shall.'

'It's the same for me.' She touched his lips, loved him with her eyes and her heart and her whole being. 'I've not had a relationship since we split up because I never wanted anyone else.'

'Oh, my love!' He hugged her to him. 'No wonder we were both so desperate.'

'You mean it's been the same for you?' she asked wonderingly.

He reached behind her and turned off the water so that his words seemed to carry even more weight in the ensuing silence. 'I've not slept with a woman in the past five years. I've not wanted to.'

'Oh, Adam, I don't know what to say…' Tears welled into her eyes and he laughed as he bent and kissed her.

'It means I have an awful lot of lost time to make up for so how about if we make a start on catching up? My bedroom or yours?'

'I don't have a bedroom, remember. I'm not supposed to be here. I should be thirty thousand feet up in the air at this precise moment.'

'Then we must do something to rectify that.'

'You don't mean you're going to send me back to England at this point!'

'Certainly not. I was thinking more along the lines of

transporting you to dizzying heights by some means other than flying.'

He stepped out of the shower stall and grabbed a towel off the rack, wrapping it around his waist before taking another one and draping it around her. Kasey smiled as he helped her out of the stall.

'Sometimes, Adam Chandler, you have the most wonderful ideas.'

'Only sometimes?' he queried, his brows arching as he opened the bathroom door.

'Yes. I don't want you getting too big for your boots by being overly lavish with the compliments.'

'Heaven forbid!' He stole another kiss as she passed him then smiled at her. 'I don't think there's any need to worry. You seem to know how to keep me in my place.'

His eyes were so full of love that her heart caught as she smiled up at him. 'And that place is with me, Adam.'

'It's the only place I want to be.'

'I wish we could stay a bit longer.'

Adam smiled when he heard the wistful note in Kasey's voice. It was the last day of their stay in Mwuranda and they were in the process of clearing up. The crew had finished dismantling the theatre tent and it was now on its way to the airfield where it would be loaded on board the plane that was due to arrive the following morning.

Two weeks had passed since the attack on the airfield and the army now had the situation under control. The rebel fighters had been driven out of the area and the town was being rebuilt. So many of the old staff had returned to the hospital that they'd been able to open another two wards, and there'd also been rumours that several of the doctors who'd fled the country were returning. Mwuranda was gradually settling down and Adam had to admit to feeling a great sense of satisfaction at what they'd achieved.

'So do I but we have to go back home at some point.' He put his arms around Kasey, ignoring the laughing looks the other members of the team exchanged. He loved her and he certainly wasn't going to try and hide his feelings.

'I know and it will be lovely to go back to England but I just wish…' She stopped and he frowned.

'You wish—what?'

'You'll think I'm crazy,' she warned him.

'But I'll love you anyway,' he told her, chuckling when she glared at him.

'Cheek!'

'I know, and I'll apologise for it later,' he promised suggestively, loving the fact that she could still blush despite the fact that they'd spent every waking and sleeping moment together for the past two weeks.

'I'll hold you to that,' she told him, but he felt the shiver that passed through her and knew how she felt.

'So tell me what's on your mind.'

'I just wish we could get married here,' she blurted out. 'Oh, I know it's a crazy idea because we said we'd have a big wedding for all our friends and family back home, but it would be so special to hold the ceremony here, wouldn't it?'

'It would,' he said slowly, because maybe it wasn't such a crazy idea after all. He, too, would love to make his vows right here in this country where they'd finally found happiness again, but would it be possible to arrange a wedding at such short notice?

'Do you really mean it?' he said briskly, because there was only one way to find out if he could make her dream come true.

'Yes, of course I do!'

'Then let's see what we can do about it.'

'But we're leaving in the morning…'

'Which means we have the rest of the day to sort everything out.' He glanced at his watch then kissed her quickly on the lips and ran to the Jeep. 'You find something to wear and I'll do the rest. Be ready in an hour. OK?'

'But, Adam…!' Kasey protested then gave up because he wasn't listening. She stared after the Jeep as he drove away, wondering what on earth he intended to do. There was no way he could arrange for them to be married in an hour's time!

Could he?

She turned and ran back into the hostel. June was in the storeroom, helping to pack up the rest of their supplies, and she looked up when Kasey raced into the room.

'What's the rush?'

'Adam…well, Adam says that we can get married. Today.'

'Today?' June's jaw dropped. 'How? I mean you can't arrange a wedding in a couple of hours. It takes months of planning and organising and—'

'If Adam says it's going to happen, I believe him. And that means I need something to wear because I am *not* getting married in a pair of jeans!'

'Right. Let's get ourselves into town and see what we can find for you.'

June quickly rallied, abandoning the cartons as she headed for the door. Katie and Lorraine were in the hall and she summoned them over and told them what was happening. Within minutes they were on their way to town and heading for the local market where June made straight for one of the stalls that sold cloth.

'See if you fancy any of these patterns,' she instructed. Kasey obediently browsed through the rolls of brightly coloured fabric until she found one in a glorious mixture of emerald green and turquoise. 'This is gorgeous.'

'We'll take it,' June told the stallholder, getting into her stride now that her initial surprise was fading.

Kasey watched in bemusement while a length of fabric was cut and paid for then they all hurried back to the hospital and headed straight for Matthias's room. Sarah was there and she was delighted to offer her help when June explained what they wanted her to do and why.

Half an hour later Kasey stood in front of the mirror and stared at herself in amazement. Sarah had fashioned for her one of the traditional dresses the local women wore, using safety-pins and lengths of tape to hold it all together. The beautiful fabric draped softly over her shoulders and was cinched in at her waist before cascading to the floor. It was the most fabulous gown she had ever worn and she was thrilled with it and said so.

'Thank you so much. It's just wonderful. I can't believe that's me in the mirror.'

'You look beautiful, Kasey,' Sarah said sincerely. 'But it isn't the gown that is making you glow like that. It's love.'

'I know. I love Adam so much…' She broke off and hugged herself because she felt she was going to burst with happiness.

June laughed as she gave her a hug as well. 'I am so pleased for you both but you certainly put us all through the mill before you got your act together!'

Everyone laughed at that. Kasey glanced round when the door opened and Florence suddenly appeared. She was holding a huge bunch of tropical flowers which she shyly handed to Kasey.

'We have picked these for you, Kasey. We all hope that you and Dr Adam are very happy together.'

'Thank you so much!' Kasey hugged her then took the

flowers from her and stared in delight at the brilliant colours. 'They are so beautiful, aren't they?'

'They are. And maybe just a couple in your hair would add the finishing touch...' Sarah plucked a couple of bright red flowers out of the bunch and pinned them into Kasey's dark curls, adding an even more exotic look to her wedding outfit.

'I just hope Adam has managed to sort everything out after all the trouble you've gone to,' she said mistily.

'I have.'

Suddenly Adam was there as well and Kasey swung round, seeing the love that lit his eyes when he looked at her in the beautiful flowing dress.

'You look beautiful,' he said softly, taking her hands and kissing them.

'Thank you.' She smiled at him, all the love she felt for him reflected in her eyes.

'Ahem! I hate to butt in but have you managed to organise this wedding or not?'

Adam grinned when June reminded them that they had an audience. 'Sorry, but you can't blame me for getting a little carried away. And, yes, I have managed to sort it out.'

'You have?' Kasey gasped. 'How?'

'I went to the orphanage and enlisted Claire's help because I thought she might be able to suggest something.'

'And did she?' she asked excitedly.

'Yes. She suggested that I have a word with Father Michael and ask him to conduct the service. He's visiting the orphanage at the moment so the timing couldn't have been better. Anyway, I asked him if he would marry us and he agreed.'

'He did!'

'Yes. Sister Beatrice very kindly offered to hold the service in their chapel so it's all arranged. I'm not sure if the marriage will be legal in England but we can check that out when we get home. It's not that important, is it? The important thing is that the wedding can take place in an hour's time if that's what you want.'

'Oh, I do. More than anything!'

'Good.' He grinned at her then turned to June. 'Can you let everyone know what's happening? The truck's outside so anyone who wants to come along is very welcome.'

'That's probably everyone,' June said with a laugh. 'After all the trials and tribulations you two went through to reach this point I expect we all want to enjoy the happy ending.'

June bustled away and the others went with her. Kasey sighed as the door closed and she and Adam were alone again. 'It's like a dream come true.'

'It's better than that because I never, ever dreamt I could be this happy.' He kissed her softly on the mouth then took hold of her hand. 'I just need to go back to the hostel and change then we can be on our way. We don't want to keep Father Michael waiting, do we?'

'No, we don't.'

She let him lead her from the room. He'd parked the Jeep in front of the hospital and she laughed when she realised that news of their wedding must have spread like wildfire because there were people hanging out of every window, waiting to wave them off. It didn't take long to get back to the hostel and she waited downstairs while Adam changed into clean trousers and a shirt. When he reappeared a short time later, she went to meet him, plucking a flower from her bouquet and tucking it into his breast pocket.

The journey to the orphanage was completed in a haze of happiness. The rest of the team had gone on ahead and were standing outside, waiting with Claire and the nuns for them to arrive. The children were also there and Kasey felt a lump come to her throat when she saw their smiling little faces as Adam helped her out of the Jeep. It made the day even more special to have them there.

The tiny chapel was ablaze with candles when they went inside and the scent of incense filled the air. Kasey held Adam's hand as they walked up the aisle together and knew that this moment would live in her heart for ever. Father Michael was standing at the altar, smiling benignly at them as he began the service, his sonorous voice making the ancient words even more beautiful.

Kasey stood in front of everyone and made her vows and knew that she meant every word. She would love Adam from that day until eternity, she would never forsake him and would love him in sickness and in health. She had found the man she wanted to spend her life with and she was truly blessed because it was what he wanted, too. When the priest proclaimed them man and wife everyone clapped.

Adam turned to her and smiled with a wealth of love in his eyes as he bent to kiss her. 'I love you, Kasey,' he whispered.

'And I love you, too. Now, always and for ever more.'

0905/03a

MILLS & BOON®
Live the emotion

_Medical
romance™

BRIDE BY ACCIDENT *by Marion Lennox*

Pregnant and stranded in Australia, beautiful doctor Emma seems determined to turn Dr Devlin O'Halloran's life upside down! Except, against all the odds, she is bringing joy into his world…

A wonderfully emotional new story from award-winning author Marion Lennox.

SPANISH DOCTOR, PREGNANT NURSE
by Carol Marinelli

Dr Ciro Delgato is quick to win Nurse Harriet Farrell's guarded heart! When Harriet discovers she's pregnant, she also hears that Ciro is leaving. She pushes him away, determined he'll never find out about their child. But has she misread the situation…?

MEDITERRANEAN DOCTORS
— Passionate about life, love and medicine.

COMING HOME TO KATOOMBA *by Lucy Clark*

Head of A&E Oliver Bowan wants nothing to get in the way of seeking custody of his daughter – but distraction comes in the shape of Dr Stephanie Brooks. But Oliver claims he can never love again – and Stephanie can't live her life on the sidelines…

BLUE MOUNTAINS A&E
— Finding love in the most beautiful place of all…

On sale 7th October 2005

Available at most branches of WHSmith, Tesco, ASDA, Borders, Eason, Sainsbury's and most bookshops

Visit www.millsandboon.co.uk

researching the cure

The facts you need to know:

- **One woman in nine** in the United Kingdom will develop breast cancer during her lifetime.

- Each year **40,700** women are newly diagnosed with breast cancer and around **12,800** women will die from the disease. However, survival rates are improving, with on average 77 per cent of women still alive five years later.

- **Men can also suffer from breast cancer**, although currently they make up less than one per cent of all new cases of the disease.

Britain has one of the highest breast cancer death rates in the world. Breast Cancer Campaign wants to understand why and do something about it. Statistics cannot begin to describe the impact that breast cancer has on the lives of those women who are affected by it and on their families and friends.

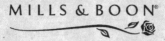

MILLS & BOON®

**During the month of October
Harlequin Mills & Boon will donate
10p from the sale of every
Modern Romance™ series book to
help Breast Cancer Campaign
in *researching the cure.***

Breast Cancer Campaign's scientific projects
look at improving diagnosis and treatment
of breast cancer, better understanding how
it develops and ultimately either curing the
disease or preventing it.

Do your part to help

Visit <u>www.breastcancercampaign.org</u>

And make a donation today.

researching the cure

Breast Cancer Campaign is a company limited by guarantee registered in England and
Wales. Company No. 05074725. Charity registration No. 299758.

FREE!

4 Books
and a surprise gift!

We would like to take this opportunity to thank you for reading this Mills & Boon® book by offering you the chance to take FOUR more specially selected titles from the Medical Romance™ series absolutely FREE! We're also making this offer to introduce you to the benefits of the Reader Service™—

- ★ **FREE home delivery**
- ★ **FREE gifts and competitions**
- ★ **FREE monthly Newsletter**
- ★ **Exclusive Reader Service offers**
- ★ **Books available before they're in the shops**

Accepting these FREE books and gift places you under no obligation to buy, you may cancel at any time, even after receiving your free shipment. Simply complete your details below and return the entire page to the address below. You don't even need a stamp!

YES! Please send me 4 free Medical Romance books and a surprise gift. I understand that unless you hear from me, I will receive 6 superb new titles every month for just £2.75 each, postage and packing free. I am under no obligation to purchase any books and may cancel my subscription at any time. The free books and gift will be mine to keep in any case.

M5ZEF

Ms/Mrs/Miss/Mr ....Initials ....

BLOCK CAPITALS PLEASE

Surname ....

Address ....

....

....Postcode ....

Send this whole page to:
UK: FREEPOST CN81, Croydon, CR9 3WZ